Also by Jessica Day George

Dragon Slippers
Dragon Flight
Dragon Spear

Tuesdays at the Castle
Wednesdays in the Tower
Thursdays with the Crown
Fridays with the Wizards
Saturdays at Sea

Sun and Moon, Ice and Snow

Princess of the Midnight Ball
Princess of Glass
Princess of the Silver Woods

Silver in the Blood

Jessica Day George

BLOOMSBURY
CHILDREN'S BOOKS
NEW YORK   LONDON   OXFORD   NEW DELHI   SYDNEY

BLOOMSBURY CHILDREN'S BOOKS
Bloomsbury Publishing Inc., part of Bloomsbury Publishing Plc
1385 Broadway, New York, NY 10018

BLOOMSBURY, BLOOMSBURY CHILDREN'S BOOKS, and the Diana logo
are trademarks of Bloomsbury Publishing Plc

First published in the United States of America in May 2018
by Bloomsbury Children's Books

Bloomsbury books may be purchased for business or promotional use. For information on
bulk purchases please contact Macmillan Corporate and Premium Sales Department at
specialmarkets@macmillan.com

Library of Congress Cataloging-in-Publication Data
Names: George, Jessica Day.
Title: The Rose legacy / by Jessica Day George.
Description: New York : Bloomsbury, 2018.
Summary: Orphaned Anthea Thornley hopes to finally find a home with her
long-lost uncle, but she soon learns not only that he secretly breeds forbidden horses,
but that she can communicate with them.
Identifiers: LCCN 2017034364 (print) • LCCN 2017045618 (e-book)
ISBN 978-1-59990-647-8 (hardcover) • ISBN 978-1-68119-694-7 (e-book)
Subjects: | CYAC: Fantasy. | Human-animal communication—Fiction. | Horses—Fiction. |
Orphans—Fiction. | Uncles—Fiction.
Classification: LCC PZ7.G293317 Ro 2018 (print) | LCC PZ7.G293317 (e-book) |
DDC [Fic]—dc23
LC record available at https://lccn.loc.gov/2017034364

Book design by John Candell
Typeset by Westchester Publishing Services
Printed and bound in the U.S.A. by Berryville Graphics Inc., Berryville, Virginia
2 4 6 8 10 9 7 5 3 1

All papers used by Bloomsbury Publishing Plc are natural, recyclable products made from wood
grown in well-managed forests. The manufacturing processes conform to the environmental
regulations of the country of origin.

To find out more about our authors and books visit www.bloomsbury.com and sign up
for our newsletters.

To everyone, including myself, who ever sat on the
arm of a sofa and shouted "Giddyup!"
To everyone, including myself, who tied a jump rope to
the handlebars of their bike, and cried out, "Whoa!"

BAD NEWS

ANTHEA BREATHED ON THE cold window, fogging the glass, and wrote her name on the misty pane. *Anthea Genevia Thornley.* Jean, the upstairs maid, would have a devil of a time getting rid of the streaks, but Anthea didn't care. Maybe Jean wouldn't notice, and ever after when the window fogged, Anthea's name would reappear.

Anthea had known it would only be a matter of time before she was shunted off to another set of relatives. Nobody wanted her for very long, although they were all very polite about it. It would not have occurred to them not to be, any more than it would have occurred to them to refuse to take her in. And it wasn't as though she were a financial burden: her parents had left her a substantial inheritance. Somehow, though, she always seemed to be in the way.

She had lived with Uncle Daniel and Aunt Deirdre for three years now, the longest she had ever stayed anywhere. But Anthea could see in the frozen expression on Aunt Deirdre's face lately that she was searching for some way to get rid of the unwanted girl.

"A new baby ought to do the trick," Anthea muttered, her breath misting the glass to complete opacity. "At least I don't have to stay on as an unpaid nurse."

One of her mother's cousins had used her as a maid of all work when she was hardly big enough to carry a coal scuttle. Anthea had been more than willing to be "sacked" for her poor silver-polishing skills. After that there was a second cousin whose son had pinched Anthea black and blue until she had slapped him in retaliation . . . and so on and so on.

Uncle Daniel was a dutiful sort who frequently apologized for not taking her in sooner. He had been the ambassador to Kronenhof for most of Anthea's life. But when he had returned to Coronam and the city of Travertine, Anthea had been unceremoniously dumped on his doorstep. Aunt Anne had "put up with" Anthea for nearly a year, she told her brother bitterly, and wasn't about to do it another minute.

"Oooh, Anthea! Jean's going to be so angry with you!"

Anthea turned to see her cousin Belinda Rose standing in the door of the bedroom they shared, her navy skirt and sailor blouse still looking fresh and pressed and her eyes round as she looked at the streaks on the window. Anthea straightened her own blouse and then transferred the frown to her cousin.

"Are you going to tattle?"

"I might," Belinda Rose said in a silky voice. "Or you could do my arithmetic . . ."

Anthea snorted. "I'd rather wash the window," she said, putting her hands to her hips. "Go on and tattle! I'll tell Aunt Deirdre that you were going to cheat."

Belinda Rose put out her lower lip, pouting and thinking at the same time. "Oh, all right!" She flounced off. "Papa wants to see you in the library," she called over her shoulder.

Grumbling, Anthea swatted at her own serge skirt, trying to restore the pleats. She was sure that her cousin had dawdled all the way so that Anthea would be scolded for tardiness.

Downstairs, Anthea knocked on the library door. The leather-upholstered book-filled room was her uncle's sanctuary, and the children were only summoned within when they were in trouble. Which meant that, despite her best efforts, Anthea was summoned to the library at least twice a month.

"Enter."

Anthea took her place on the Kronenhofer rug in front of her uncle's desk. She clasped her hands at her waist and put her shoulders back, head high. She was trying for the exact pose depicted in the portrait of Princess Jennet that hung in the entrance of her school.

Uncle Daniel sat back in his large desk chair, his fingers

steepled under his chin, and studied her. He did not seem impressed. Anthea sagged just a little.

Even though it was highly improper, she spoke first. "Belinda Rose has already told me the news."

"I'm sorry, I didn't want you to hear it from her first." He frowned. "And I must speak to her about tattling."

That gave Anthea a pang, since her cousin had just told her that she would not tattle. But then Anthea sighed, because it didn't matter, really. She would be packed and out the door before Belinda Rose had time to think of a suitable revenge.

"At any rate, Anthea, I *am* sorry about this." Uncle Daniel's face was strained. "It's just that Deirdre and I didn't expect to have any more children. It has come as rather a shock, and necessitated a few . . . adjustments."

"That's all right, Uncle," she managed to say.

She didn't enjoy being lumped into the adjustments, which also included moving a cradle into Elizabeth Rose's room. No one liked feeling like furniture. Anthea didn't comment on that, however, but steeled herself to ask the question that was really troubling her.

"But where will I go? I thought I had exhausted the hospitality of every one of my relations by now."

She grimaced. She didn't mean to be a burden, but since no one wanted her to begin with, they were only too happy to find a reason to get rid of her. It didn't seem to matter how good her grades were, or what awards she won, or how polite and eager to please she was at home. She was an inconvenience no matter what she did.

Her uncle gave her a pained smile. "Yes, er, that's really what I wanted to speak to you about. There is, I'm afraid, only one other option." He straightened the row of silver pencils on his desk. "It was Deirdre's idea, which is surprising . . . ," he muttered.

Anthea crossed her fingers and silently prayed that the only option wouldn't prove to be a spinster aunt who smelled of mothballs and liked to have the death notices in the paper read aloud to her every afternoon.

"You see"—Uncle Daniel cleared his throat and brought her attention back to him—"there really is no flaw in your character. You're an amiable enough young lady, not without looks and charm . . . brains for certain. I wish Belinda Rose had half your . . . but no matter. Your father left you with ample finances as well, and I know you dream of taking up the Rose before you marry . . . a worthy goal indeed." He paused, sighed, pursed his lips, and looked up at the ceiling.

"Then why does no one want me?" The question burst from her lips before she could stop it. She clenched her teeth to stop a sob from following.

Uncle Daniel, to his credit, didn't bother to argue, but looked at her gravely. "Do you know what your father's occupation was?"

The question took her off guard and stopped the tears

before they could fall. "Not really," Anthea admitted. "Actually, not at all."

She had long ago deduced that her father had not been very highly placed in society. After all, everywhere Uncle Daniel went there were men who shook his hand and spoke in reverent tones of his work with the Foreign Office. But never once had Anthea encountered someone who knew her father.

Anthea drew herself up nevertheless and remembered that her mother would never have married someone who wasn't of great importance. Before her marriage, Genevia Cross had been a Favored Rose Maiden. The queen herself had arranged the Cross-Thornley marriage.

"Your father managed his family's estate," Uncle Daniel said, his voice clipped. "It's in a rather ... unfashionable ... location. Quite out-of-the-way, one might say.

"His brother, Andrew Thornley, is now the owner. He'll be your new guardian."

"I see."

But she didn't. She had never heard of Andrew Thornley, had not known she had an uncle on her father's side, but Uncle Daniel had begun to speak again.

"He writes that he is thrilled to have you." Uncle Daniel frowned down at a letter on his desk.

Anthea found this highly unlikely; no one was ever thrilled to have her. But it was nice of him to say so. It boded well for the next few months.

"You will leave in two days," Uncle Daniel went on. "Your uncle will meet you at the train station outside the Wall."

"The Wall?" One of her hands rose to the collar of her blouse. "*Kalabar's* Wall? You're sending me to live near the Wall?"

Uncle Daniel rolled his silver pencils beneath his palm. "Not quite. The estate is some distance beyond it, I understand."

Anthea felt the ground heave beneath her feet. Her voice came out as a whisper. "*Beyond* the Wall? In the Exiled Lands?" Her knees were shaking as Uncle Daniel merely gave her a nod in answer.

Without asking permission, Anthea sank down into one of the high-backed leather chairs. The Exiled Lands! That was where the Crown sent traitors, pagans, and other undesirables! She had heard stories from the girls at school who came from northern Coronam. They said that the exiles ate unspeakable things, like raw meat and goat eyeballs. And the women wore trousers while the men wore skirts, but nobody wore drawers at all!

"I'm very sorry."

Her uncle looked sorry. In fact, his face looked lined and almost old, though he was not yet forty. Anthea wondered how much pressure her aunt had put on Uncle Daniel to force him to send his niece into exile. And how dreadful a burden was Anthea that the only option left to her was to be sent into exile herself?

"Is my uncle—my other uncle—is he—" Her throat was so dry she couldn't finish the thought, but Uncle Daniel knew what she was thinking.

"Andrew Thornley is *not* an exile," he said. "He apparently chooses to live there. He says he will explain it to you when you arrive." Uncle Daniel straightened the letter again, his mouth a thin line. "I am so sorry, Anthea. This isn't something I would wish on any young lady of breeding. But I'm afraid that I'm rather at the end of my tether. Deirdre . . ."

He was saved from having to finish that thought by Delia, the downstairs maid, who bustled in, her eyes alight with curiosity. She would be dying to get juicy details about Anthea's banishment she could carry back to the kitchen.

"Dinner is served, sir," she said, her eyes on Anthea.

"Thank you, Delia," Uncle Daniel said sharply.

With a disappointed huff, the maid backed out of the room. She valued her job too much, however, to slam the door or listen at the keyhole.

"You're a good girl, Anthea," Uncle Daniel said. "I'm sure that you'll be all right. In a few years you can look toward a ladies' college of some kind. There are none beyond the Wall, so you will be able to return to Coronam then. You might consider teaching, or nursing."

"Either of those would be nice," Anthea responded dully.

What was running through her head was that all she really wanted was to be a Rose Maiden, like her mother and her aunt

Deirdre. But would the queen select a Maiden who had lived among exiles? Her heart shuddered.

She was ruined.

"Very good," Uncle Daniel said. He seemed relieved, and Anthea realized that, after years of living with Aunt Deirdre, he'd expected her to have hysterics. "You'll be back in civilized society before you know it." He gave her a slight smile. "Anthea?"

"Thank you," she managed.

"You are welcome. You may be excused."

THE LONG ROAD NORTH

"OI, REDGE! YOU TOSSER!"

"What? I din't do nuffin!"

"Tha's the point! Mite of a schoolgirl in car two din't get put out at Blackham!"

"I tried! Din't her ticket say the Wall? Din't it just!"

"Cor! Did it?"

"It did! Plain as brass!"

"Never heard th'like. She an exile, then?"

"Too young, in't she?"

"Dunno."

Anthea shut out the conductors' voices with an effort. She opened her book, *Lives of the Crown*, and set it down again. Miss Miniver, the headmistress of her school, had given it to her as a going-away present. In her precise, angular hand the headmistress had written on the frontispiece: *"Let these worthy examples guide you in lawless lands,*" but Anthea wasn't in the mood to read stories of piety and sacrifice.

She was restless, but there was nowhere to go, save up and down the narrow aisle of the train. But this activity seemed to be largely favored by men with cigars, and not young ladies, so Anthea didn't dare to try it. Outside the grimy windows, field after field passed by, the monotonous green broken only by a quick glimpse of the occasional town or village. In the beginning there had been frequent stops at bustling stations, with passengers getting on and off and luggage being loaded and unloaded amid gusts of steam from the engine and shouts from the porters.

But everyone in her car had disembarked at the last station, and no one new had gotten on at all. The conductor had been shocked to find her still sitting there and demanded to see her ticket; he was certain that she had forgotten to get off somewhere farther south. There were no more stations left until they reached the Wall, where the train customarily delivered only mail before turning around for the long trek back to the south and civilized society.

Anthea breathed on the window and wrote her name in the foggy patch. Streaking windows with her name would be her way of leaving a mark on the world. Now that it seemed she would have no chance to leave a better one.

If she didn't freeze to death in some hovel, as Belinda Rose gleefully predicted, then her reputation would be ruined. Permanently. Belinda Rose had been sworn to secrecy by her parents, but Anthea knew by the gleam in her cousin's eyes that everyone at Miss Miniver's Rose Academy would know Anthea's fate within a day, a week at the most.

It was dark outside the train now. The green of the fields was gray and black in the moonlight, and Anthea could hardly tell the difference between a barn and a grove of trees. She opened the hamper at her feet and pulled out the last of the sandwiches that Mrs. Murch, Uncle Daniel's cook, had packed for her.

Anthea ate the final sandwich—cold chicken with pickle—and drank the bitter tea. The cake was stale, so she nibbled the icing and candied cherries off the top and left the rest. Then she noticed something sticking out from under the napkin lining the bottom of the hamper. Lifting aside the napkin, she found a letter in what was unmistakably Aunt Deirdre's hand.

Anthea unfolded the note slowly. She wasn't sure she wanted to be treated to a sermon on remembering her place or avoiding foreign customs just now. Something slithered out of the letter and landed in her lap, glinting in the compartment's lamp.

Startled, Anthea looked at it for a long time before she realized that it was a silver pendant on a silver chain. And not just any pendant: a Royal Coronami Rose, set with a small pearl at its heart.

The Royal Family had ruled Coronam for a thousand years. Princess Jennet, the sister of King Aloster IV, had been the model of all that was good and lovely in a young lady. She had been not only beautiful but intelligent and pious, and so her symbol of the rose had become treasured by all young ladies who aspired to Princess Jennet's example. Jennet had refused to marry so that she might spend her days waiting upon her sister-in-law, Queen Lythia, and had founded the Society of Rose Maidens.

Anthea had always admired the gold-and-garnet rose necklace that Belinda Rose had been given on her last birthday. Anthea set the letter aside and lifted this one. The silver rose was just as finely engraved as her cousin's, and the pearl was a beautiful soft gray, which would suit Anthea's gray eyes. She clasped it around her neck and resolved to try to live up to the example of Princess Jennet, no matter how dire her circumstances.

Then she picked up the letter to read.

My dear niece,

I am so desperately sorry for the grave trial that has been placed before you. But you have always been such a model of gracious behavior that I am sure you shall pass through this time and emerge unscathed, an example to us all.

And remember: if you ever have need of someone to confide in, please confide in me! I will anxiously await all your news.

Your doting aunt,
Deirdre August-Cross, R. M.

Anthea let her hands, holding the letter, fall to her lap. She hardly knew how to feel about this letter. Her *doting* aunt Deirdre? Anthea found her aunt's letter very odd. Aunt Deirdre had never had a compliment for her when Anthea was living under her roof.

Frowning, Anthea read the letter twice more, then she folded it and stuck it between the pages of her book. She would worry about it later, she decided. For now, she had other things to occupy her mind.

The train was slowing down. They had reached the Wall.

STRANGE NEW WORLD

ALL CORONAMI CHILDREN LEARNED of the great plague that decimated their kingdom—a plague caused by creatures called horses that the backward northern people used instead of oxen. The plague had killed off most of the horses, along with thousands of people, yet the northerners refused to destroy the rest of the infected animals. King Kalabar, the Great Defender, built the Wall to create a barrier between civilized folk and the northerners and their animals, which soon died anyway. In the centuries since, any unwanted elements that had plagued Coronam had been exiled beyond its massive stones. And now Anthea was joining them.

The Wall itself was tall and rough and forbidding, she found as she disembarked at the tiny station. The only other thing for miles around, besides the gatehouse, was the small train station. Both were made of the same dark-gray stone as the Wall.

Two mailbags were handed to the stationmaster, a taciturn man in a worn blue suit, and two mailbags were given to the porter in turn. He loaded them onto the train, deposited Anthea's trunk at her feet, tipped his cap, and left. The stationmaster also tipped his cap to her, then took the mail inside the station house and closed the door.

It was dark and cold. Anthea pulled her coat—best navy-blue wool with staghorn buttons, as required for those attending Miss Miniver's—closer around her and stamped her feet in their leather boots to keep her blood flowing. Her uncle Andrew knew she was coming; after all, he had purchased her ticket! Why was no one here to meet her?

After an interminable amount of time that the station clock somehow only marked as half an hour, she decided to force her way into the station house. But then she heard a growling and clanking that seemed to indicate a vehicle was coming.

"Finally!" Anthea exclaimed, then schooled her expression into polite patience, as though she weren't cold and tired and worried.

Into the circle of lantern light came a vehicle of dubious origin. Anthea could not tell if it was merely very, very old or cobbled together out of spare parts or both. It seemed to be some sort of motorcar, but between the mismatched wheels and the wooden cart bench that served as a seat, she wasn't actually sure.

It pulled up alongside the platform. The man driving

clucked his tongue and then looked around, said "Whoa!" and finally turned off the engine.

"Not my first choice, but it does in a pinch!"

It took Anthea a moment to sort through his accent. Then she had to avert her eyes as he clambered up on the platform beside her. From the waist up he was dressed like a country gentleman in a felted jacket, white shirt, and knitted tie, with a hat bearing a small cockade of brown feathers. But below that he only wore a scarlet kilt, which showed his gnarled knees above gray wool socks and thick-soled ankle boots.

"Bit tired, Miss Thea?" The man said it with real concern, cocking his head to one side as he studied her downturned face. "Terrible journey, I'm sure. Here."

Before she could protest, he leaped down to the cobblestones again, grabbed her by the waist, and swung her onto the seat of the car. She sat, stunned, while he put her trunk, hamper, and the satchel containing her books into the wooden-sided back of the contraption.

The gnarled man hopped nimbly onto the seat beside her while she was still arranging her coat around her. He pressed the starter and jiggled the wheel, clucking his tongue. He pumped the pedals and pressed the starter again. The odd little car coughed and shuddered but didn't move.

"This isnae my sort of travel," the man said.

"You have to . . . you put your foot on . . ."

Anthea stopped, flustered. She knew she shouldn't

contradict her elders, but Miss Miniver had made sure that her students could all operate a motorcar, in case they were ever without a professional driver for some reason.

"Ah, that's the thing!"

The man finally got the car started, and they lurched forward. All Anthea could do was hang on as the rackety machine was turned around and headed for the gate in the Wall.

"Don't remember me, do ye?" the man shouted over the noise of the engine.

"I beg your pardon?"

"Don't remember me, eh? Eh?"

"I'm afraid I don't," Anthea admitted. She searched the weathered profile. "Should I? Sir?"

"I'm Caillin MacRennie," he said. "And that's why everyone calls me Caillin MacRennie!" He laughed. "I knew ye when ye were no more'n a babby."

"You did?" This information drew even more of Anthea's attention from the blackness of the Wall looming ahead of them. "Did you live in Bellair?"

"Bellair? Nay!" He snorted at the very idea. "Never been farther south than Blackham in my life!"

"Then I'm afraid that you are mistaken, sir," Anthea said as they stopped at the gatehouse in the shadow of the wall. "I've never been farther north than Harkham until today." Harkham was almost a hundred miles to the south.

"Or so they told ye," Caillin MacRennie said with another

snort before he called over to the gatehouse. "Hi, there! Comin' back through!"

"Quick enough trip," said a broad man in a gray army uniform who came out of the little stone house. "Was it even worth dusting off this old relic?"

He made as if to kick one of the tires of their vehicle, but he stopped when he saw Anthea. He tipped his cap to her.

"Evening, miss!"

"Good evening, sir," she said. "My name is Anthea Thornley." She thought that she was supposed to have some sort of paper to show, but none had been given to her. "I'm afraid I haven't any documents with me . . ."

"I know, miss," the guard said genially. "Caillin MacRennie explained everything on his way through." He tipped his cap again. "Welcome home, miss."

"Um, thank you . . . ?" Anthea was too tired to find a nice way to correct him.

"Oh, and here," the guard said. He handed Anthea a small brown paper bag. "A little something to appease those monsters at the farm," he said with a wink and a theatrical shudder.

"Pardon?" Anthea let the bag slither off her lap onto the floor of the car. "The . . . monsters?"

"Ought to come see the monsters," Caillin MacRennie said. "They could thank ye for the sugar in person!"

"We'll see," the guard said with false sincerity. "But I feel like once was more than enough."

Both men laughed as the iron portcullis clanked upward. The little car passed through the stone tunnel that led from Kalabar's Wall into the wilderness, and Anthea gripped the wooden edge of her seat tightly, the bag of sugar cubes forgotten at her feet.

"So these are the Exiled Lands," she said, trying to distract herself.

"Or Leana, as we call it," Caillin MacRennie replied dryly. "Welcome back, Miss Thea."

"Leana? I thought that was just a myth," Anthea said, her voice faint. "I'm afraid that I've never been here either way. You must be mistaken about having known me as a babb— baby, sir."

Caillin MacRennie let out a braying laugh. "I'm no so old! What lies have they been feeding ye down south, anyway? You're Leanan born: Why d'ye think ye didn't need any festerin' papers to leave the precious Crown lands?"

Anthea simply could not let his disparaging tone go unpunished. She drew herself upright on the hard seat. "Coronam is my home, sir, and even on this side of Kalabar's Wall, she is still your sovereign nation! I find your disrespectful tone in extremely poor taste."

Caillin MacRennie did not comment on this but pushed hard on one of the pedals to make the car jolt along faster. They rode in silence for quite a while, through a dark countryside not much different from that on the other side of the Wall.

Anthea soon deflated, however, knowing that she had been altogether too abrupt, even rude. Still, she had been in the right to take him to task for his unpatriotic comment, so she did not apologize. But she did ask about the lights.

They had passed a few lights here and there: farmhouses, she had guessed. The occasional public building even. But ahead of them was a glow that looked like it came from more than just a single lantern or farmhouse window.

"That'd be Last Farm," he said.

"The last farm?" she repeated, puzzled.

Caillin MacRennie didn't answer, but he smiled. He cranked the wheel and they turned up a long lane. It was narrow but smoothly paved, and tall posts hung with lanterns had been placed all along it. Beyond the pools of light were wide pastures.

There were animals in some of the pastures. Large ones, but the light wasn't strong enough for Anthea to see if they were oxen or merely cows. She could hear the voices of men calling out as they moved among the animals, herding them toward a long, low building that was unlike any barn she had ever seen.

It had brightly lit windows and was made of gray stone. As she peered through the dimness at it, she caught the scent of hay and something else. Oats? She had never really thought about what oats smelled like, outside of porridge. But now she could smell them, almost taste them. And she felt warm, even though a chill drizzle was falling.

The feeling of warmth, the taste of oats and hay, it all grew around Anthea until she thought she would choke on it. There was a smell, too, a smell that reminded her of something, but she couldn't think what. She wasn't sure if the smell was pleasant or unpleasant, but she put her handkerchief over her nose and mouth all the same.

A tremble began in her hands and spread up her arms and down her legs. At last the motorcar reached a wide cobbled courtyard in front of an enormous, rambling manor house. It had a high slate roof and a wide front door painted bright blue.

The elegant appearance of the manor took Anthea by surprise, to say the least. So, too, did the inhuman scream that came from off to the right, beyond one of the white fences. Anthea's head whipped around, and she saw a massive shape rear up, far taller than a man, in the darkness.

"Wh-wh-what is it?" Anthea said.

"Oh, just Con sayin' hello," said Caillin MacRennie. "Or rather, sayin' it's his land, and you smell diff'rent."

"Con? But what *is* it?"

Because now, in the light of the lamps, Anthea could make out other shapes. Men were moving around in the fields, along with animals, massive things that she couldn't quite see clearly in the darkness.

The wind carried more scents to her: Grass. Muddy earth. And that other smell. The smell of these animals. Memories began to stir in her brain. Con screamed again.

"Horses. Those are horses," Anthea said faintly.

"O'course they are," Caillin MacRennie said, and laughed. "What did you think they were: rats?"

"They're supposed to be *dead*," Anthea said.

"Now, who told you that?" Caillin MacRennie said.

"Everyone," Anthea said. "Everyone knows. The diseases. The plagues."

She pressed her handkerchief even more tightly over her mouth. How soon would they make her sick?

"Miss Thea? Are you all right?"

Before she could even think of how to answer, a tall, broad-shouldered man came out of the manor to meet them. He had thick brown hair, gray at the temples, and was quite handsome. He looked so very familiar, in a way that was much more welcome than the horses.

With a little sob, Anthea flung herself out of the cart and into his arms.

"Oh, Papa! Help me," she wailed.

The man hugged her for a moment, and then he gently held her out at arm's length. "It's me, your uncle Andrew," he said kindly. "Welcome back to Last Farm, Thea dear."

FLORIAN

The wind curled through the evening air and wandered into the eastern paddock. It brought many scents with it: smoke from the lanterns hanging along the drive and outside the stable, men in heavy boots sweating despite the chill in the air, a coming frost, the meats and baked things that had been dinner at the Big House.

And one more smell.

One tiny thread of scent that would not cause another horse to so much as flick an ear in response. But when it reached Florian's nostrils, his entire body went rigid.

She had returned.

Over a decade's absence made no difference. Florian knew that it was she.

He smelled soap with roses in it, a hint of fresh bread, something that made him think of the color blue. Florian strained over the fence as far as he could, nostrils flared to gather in every particle of the scent, to make certain that it was not lies or madness. A voice came on the wind: older, deeper, yet hers all the same. His ears swiveled and pricked, hungry for every word.

"Come along, come along!"

A man, impatient, at his shoulder. Florian did not move. The man prodded him, trying to make him turn, but he would not move. The man climbed onto the lower rungs of the fence to reach his halter, and still Florian ignored him. He must not go to the stable, unless that was where *she* was going. He yanked his head free, and strained again to hear or see or smell where she might be. There was a commotion near the front of the Big House, but it died down quickly, and her scent faded.

Pain filled him, as sharp as it had been when she first left. Why did she not come to him? Why did she go to the Big House, where he was not? Anger followed the pain, anger at the men who he knew had pushed her away, who would not let her come to the paddock.

When the man grabbed Florian's halter, he yanked his head away, rearing and screaming in challenge. The man scrambled out of the way of Florian's hooves, and he called for help. Other men came running, but Florian ignored them. He ran to the open gate of the paddock and through it, clattering across the packed earth of the stable yard. If they would not let her come to him, he would go to her.

Before he could get to the Big House, though, another man

stepped in front of him. It was The Thornley, and Florian skidded to a stop. The Thornley was the men's herd stallion, and Florian would not disobey him. Even so, he trembled with rage and anguish while The Thornley took hold of Florian's halter and led him to the stable.

Florian bared his teeth at the man who came to feed him after The Thornley had gone, and the man gave him his oats and left. Good. Florian did not want him in the way. *She* would come to him soon, and he didn't want the man there.

Florian lipped at the oats, drank a little water, but could not settle down. When would she come?

Beloved Anthea.

At last she had returned to him.

RUDE AWAKENING

ANTHEA DECIDED TO LIE in bed until her humiliation faded from everyone's mind. Years if need be. The good news was that she would never have to unpack.

She pulled the comforter up to her nose and blocked the light coming in through the flimsy muslin curtains with her arm. The room was very pretty, now that she was looking around. It was furnished with elegant mahogany pieces; the bed was a massive four-poster with a canopy of white muslin. The dresser had a marble top and an oval mirror, and there was a fireplace with a velvet-upholstered wing chair pulled up to it. Anthea had never had her own fireplace before, let alone a big cozy chair that she could curl up in to read.

That was, if she stayed. Right now she was too humiliated. She had flung herself at her uncle like an insane person, called him Papa, and burst into tears when he corrected her. He had carried her like a child to this room, while a veritable army of rough-looking men looked on. And then a tall Kirbinish woman in a starched apron had undressed her, given her a sponge bath, and put her in a strange nightgown. Embarrassed almost beyond words, Anthea had tried to protest, but the woman merely smiled and kept on washing her.

It went beyond humiliation now that she thought of it again. She would have to leave. There was no way she could face her uncle and his people.

And to make everything so much worse, the fields outside were full of horses.

"You're awake!" a voice called from the doorway. "Finally! I've been waiting *hours!*"

Anthea didn't recognize the voice. It was female, but young—not the woman from last night. Was there another young lady in residence? Had she witnessed Anthea's behavior of the night before?

Anthea's cheeks flamed again, and she almost pulled the comforter over her head. Almost, but not quite. The other girl knew she was here; hiding would only compound Anthea's list of embarrassing behaviors.

Tentatively, Anthea raised herself out of the nest of bedding. Standing at the foot of the bed was a girl about her own age, with huge blue eyes and a tousled mass of curly brown hair so short that it didn't even reach her chin. She was clad in an outlandish suit of clothing that Anthea realized after a moment was a pair of *men's* pajamas—of maroon paisley silk! There was rouge on her cheeks, and the pajama pants were tucked into a pair of shiny black boots like the kind that soldiers wore. Forgetting her determination to act like a young lady, Anthea simply gaped.

"It's really you!" the girl squealed, and then jumped over the footboard and onto the bed, boots and all. Anthea barely drew her legs back in time to avoid being crushed. "At last! I've missed you so much!" And the girl threw her arms around Anthea's neck and planted a kiss on her cheek.

Yet another person who thought that she had known Anthea before!

Anthea drew back from the girl's embrace. "I am sorry," she said, with the firm tone that Miss Miniver had taught her pupils to use when speaking to overly forward strangers. "But I'm afraid you are mistaken. I would surely remember if we had ever met before."

The other girl looked baffled by Anthea's stiff reply.

"Of course we've met! Don't you remember sneaking into each other's rooms at night? And the first time Daddy put us on a horse? We both got to sit on Constantine together! But now I'm not even allowed to *touch* Con," she chattered on. "No one can, except Finn, but he still can't ride him. Con's the herd stallion since Justinian died, and I can't wait for you to see him! We can look even if we can't pet . . ." The girl trailed off when she saw Anthea's horrified expression.

"I must insist that you please get off my bed and introduce yourself properly," Anthea said in a strangled voice. "I have no idea who you think I am or who you are. But I am used to . . ."

Anthea trailed off. It was true that she was used to much more formal introductions when she entered a new household, but that was mainly because they weren't all that eager to make her acquaintance. This girl, on the other hand . . .

The strangely dressed girl slithered off the bed and landed on the rug with a thump of her boots. She was staring at Anthea as though Anthea had two heads, and a high color that clashed with the rouge she wore had risen in her face. Her mouth opened and closed several times before she managed to choke out, "It's me! Jilly! Jillian? *Your cousin?* We were born on the same day, Thea! What happened to you?"

"I became a young lady," Anthea said, and she couldn't help but let her eyes linger on Jilly's short hair and her wildly inappropriate costume.

"You became *something*," Jilly said. She stormed out of the room, slamming the door behind her.

The slam was like a pitcher of cold water being dashed in Anthea's face. She dodged her shame and went to the window, ducking under the curtains, and gazed out at the farm.

Horses. Everywhere. Her jaw fell open as she looked at them for the first time in full daylight. Horses and nothing else, save the men caring for them. Anthea couldn't see a single cow or pig or chicken on the farm. Only horses.

How could there be so many of them?

Squares of white-painted wooden fencing separated groups of russet and deep-brown, black, gray, and flame-red horses, gleaming in the early morning sunlight. Men in tall boots moved among them, slapping their sides, stroking the long hair that hung down the beasts' narrow faces, strapping on harnesses, leaping onto broad backs. They treated them as casually as Uncle Daniel's driver had treated their motorcar, rubbing them with cloths, moving them back and forth, talking and whistling as they went about their work.

None of the people or animals looked sickly, but how could Anthea be sure? She couldn't remember ever reading an exact description of the plague. The men seemed unconcerned, but what did that mean? Were they already sick? Did they not know about the plague?

Her breath fogged the windowpane, and she stretched out a finger to write her name, but a sound brought her up short. It was that scream again, as chilling as anything she had ever heard, primal and challenging as it rent the air. Everyone froze, not just Anthea. The men and horses below the window all turned and looked toward one of the little fenced paddocks.

It held a single horse, a massive beast, mostly a golden-brown color with a black mane and tail and black coloring across his back and shoulders like a mantle. He stretched his long neck up and screamed again, then rose onto his hind legs and pawed the air. Anthea recognized it as the creature that had frightened her last night, the one that Caillin Mac-Rennie had called Con. Jillian, too, had said something about sitting on Con, but Anthea pushed that thought away. It was clearly impossible. No sane person would have put a child atop that monster.

A shock of fear went through her when she saw Uncle Andrew duck between the rails of the fence and step into that monster's pen. He held out his arms wide, facing the angry horse with a straight back and not a hint of nerves that Anthea could detect. The horse came back down to all fours and stared at Andrew for a long, long time. Then he shook his head, pawed at the earth, and turned away as though dismissing the man. Shaking his own head, Andrew climbed back out of the paddock, gesturing to the men nearest to move their horses farther from the huge, angry creature he had just faced.

Anthea moved away from the window before anyone noticed her and went to the chair by the fireplace. She needed time to think.

Her uncle Andrew raised horses, and the people just south of the Wall had no idea they still existed. The Crown had no idea that horses still existed. And why would her uncle do such a thing? Did he want to spread the plague among the exiles? What if the disease was carried south to ravage Coronam again?

This made Anthea shudder. She was not meant for this life. She wanted finer things: a place at court as a Rose Maiden, the

King's Blessing, an elegant marriage, things that might be
beyond the grasp of any young lady who was sent to live beyond
the Wall. She clutched at the silver pendant Aunt Deirdre had
given her, thinking of what a properly trained Rose Maiden
would do in these dire circumstances.

Her aunt's letter ran through her mind: *"You have always
been such a model of gracious behavior . . ."* The words filled
her with strength. She would ignore the horses and act with
the calm dignity and graciousness of a Coronami lady, just
as Princess Jennet would have done. Perhaps she could even
train her cousin so that she wouldn't be so alone.

Yes, that would be the proper thing to do, she decided. Aunt
Deirdre and Miss Miniver could not help but approve if they
knew that she was undertaking to guide her less fortunate
cousin on the Path of the Rose. It might even help Anthea
regain her social footing, once she returned south. She could
make it sound like her reason for living beyond the Wall
had been to help this "Jilly."

Anthea rose from the chair and went to the washstand,
where fresh water had been laid on while she slept. She washed
and dressed herself in a pleated school skirt and middy, taking
special pains with the red ribbon that held her waving brown
hair at the nape of her neck and making sure that her rose pendant hung just in the center of the square sailor collar.

Throwing back her shoulders, she stepped out of the room
at last.

5

Choking on the Truth

THE MUD WAS UP to Anthea's ankles. With every step she was sucked down into the horrid stuff and had to drag her leg back out again. But she persevered, slogging across the yard in spite of the filth, heading for the paddock where she could see Uncle Andrew giving orders to six young men mounted on horses.

The sight of these enormous beasts looming closer made her heart quail. Up close they were more menacing than beautiful, their backs nearly the height of her head, but she kept on, the young man trailing behind her.

"You'll ruin your shoes," he kept saying. "Borrow some of Jilly's boots!"

"Leave me alone," Anthea said without turning around.

"Not until you stop!" the young man snapped.

"I have to talk to my uncle," she told him, and continued to fight her way through the mire. She had nearly reached her uncle when someone at another paddock even farther away called out to Andrew.

"Andrew! Over here! Something's wrong with Caesar!"

And before Anthea could get her uncle's attention, he headed off to the other paddock. In his tall boots he covered the ground much faster than Anthea could hope to, and before she knew it he was even farther away. In fact, Anthea appeared to be the only person affected by the mud at all. The boy behind her seemed to have mastered some miraculous way of walking on top of it.

But still Anthea persisted. And at last, breathless, filthy, and with aching legs, she arrived at a small paddock where her uncle looked over a large golden-red animal. The horse's head was hanging down, and it wheezed every breath.

It wasn't the only one wheezing, though. Anthea couldn't seem to get her breath, either, and for a moment she clutched at the fence and gasped. It wasn't until she coughed, trying to dispel the sudden feeling that there was a stone in her throat, that her uncle turned to look at her. For a moment he didn't seem to know who she was, then a faint smile chased the concern from his face. The smile faded as he took in the remains of her once-fresh school uniform.

"Finn should have let you change before he took you on a tour," her uncle said. "I know you probably don't have any trousers or boots yet, but Jilly has plenty. Didn't she find you yet?"

Then the horse wheezed, and Andrew went back to feeling its side, his brow clouded. Finn, looking as concerned as her uncle, stepped around Anthea to stroke the animal's long neck, murmuring to it softly.

Anthea gulped and gasped for air, trying to respond but unable to make a sound. There was something lodged in her throat! Had the damp air settled in her lungs already and made her ill? She had heard that the air north of the Wall was unhealthy, but she had been out in it for only a quarter of an hour at the most!

A jolt of icy terror went through her. Was it the plague? Had she caught it already? If she could have taken a step back from the horse, she would have, but her shoes were stuck fast.

"I don't want a tour," she managed. Her voice sounded muffled. "I'm not—don't want—to be around *horses*! And that boy says I'm to have riding lessons?"

At the sound of her voice, the horse lifted its head. It had huge brown eyes, round and long lashed, and the whites showed in a way that she somehow knew meant distress. It shifted restlessly and flicked its tail. Anthea could clearly hear the beast swallowing, or trying to swallow, and she felt the lump in her throat expand. She breathed through her nose and couldn't look away from the horse's panic-stricken eyes. She tasted oats, and with them something that was not oats. The thing that was not oats was round and squishy and was now scratchily lodged halfway down her throat . . .

No. Not *her* throat. *Its* throat. The horse's throat. Anthea was feeling light-headed now, and she held out a trembling hand to point at the horse.

"There's a sponge," she gasped. "It ate a sponge. Stupid beast." She choked and tried to cough, even though she knew it wouldn't do any good.

The boy Finn looked at her sharply. He turned to Andrew, who raised his eyebrows.

"Hold his head, John," Uncle Andrew ordered.

Uncle Andrew shoved his right sleeve as far up his arm as he could and reached into the beast's mouth while Finn held it open and the other man held the horse's head up. Andrew's eyes widened, and he slowly withdrew his arm. Clamped in his fingertips was a sponge the size of an apple.

The horse gave a great rattling gasp, and a wave of relief flowed through Anthea. Both she and the beast straightened where they stood, and the horse swallowed several times and then made a high-pitched chuckling noise. If Anthea could have made such a noise, she would have, too. The horse shook its mane, and Anthea did copy that, tossing her tail of hair over her shoulder.

Now everyone was staring at her: Uncle Andrew, John, Finn . . . even the horse. Anthea's throat was clear, but her face was red and burning.

"How did you know about the sponge?" Uncle Andrew's eyes were calculating.

A desperate urge inflamed Anthea. The urge to run, and keep running, far from here. Back to the city, back to her uncle Daniel's house, where everything was calm and clean and sane. Where there was no mud or strangers staring at her or horses.

Where she couldn't feel what a horse was feeling.

She stared back at her uncle Andrew, not knowing how to answer or if she wanted to answer. The only thing that kept her upright was her grip on the fence post. The horse leaned forward and pressed its soft nose to the back of one of her hands. It felt like a fine kid glove, and its whiskers tickled her fingers.

A horse was touching her.

Anthea reeled back with a shriek. Her feet, stuck deep in the mud, did not budge, and she fell hard into Finn. He dropped the gear he was still carrying just in time to catch her, and she half leaned, half lay against the young man for a long time, panting and staring wildly from the horse to her uncle.

"You can sense his feelings, can't you?" Her uncle's voice was gentle. He smiled faintly. "Of course you can."

"I should not be here," Anthea whispered. "Please let me go home."

Her uncle looked at her for a long time. Then he said, "We can't. You have the Way, as your father suspected. It's a rare gift, too rare to let you go. I'm sorry, Anthea, but you have to stay."

Anthea shook off Finn's hands and fled toward the house as rapidly as she could. Her thoughts raced as her shoes squelched through mud—endless mud!—but no one came after her, to her relief.

Once she got inside she couldn't remember if her room was to the right or the left. Somehow she made her way back upstairs and to her quiet, empty room. She had to be alone. She had to think.

6

HEAD STUFFED FULL

WHEN SHE WOKE, IT was evening and the room was dark. She didn't even realize she had fallen asleep until she heard the knocking on her door again.

Getting to her feet, she moved toward the door with caution. When she reached it, she put one hand on the key but didn't turn it.

"Who is it?" she called through the door.

"It's your uncle," came a weary voice. "I know this has come as quite a shock, but if I could just talk to you?"

Anthea threw open the door.

"A *shock*?" Her voice rose and she struggled to keep it level. "A shock does not begin to describe it! First I am cast out of the first real home I have had since my parents died and . . . Do you know how many . . . how *very* many houses I have lived in?"

She didn't wait for a reply. She herself had lost count, as the number had grown too painful to contemplate.

"After all the time I've spent trying to be a proper young lady. A young lady who wouldn't be a burden to others. Then I am told that I am being exiled like some common criminal! And that all the filthy horses were not wiped out by plague but are alive and I am to live surrounded by them! On a farm! And *then* I find out that I can feel what some awful horse is feeling?

"A *shock*? All I want is to be a Rose Maiden," she said, taking a great dragging breath. "I want to receive the King's Blessing. And now that will never happen."

"It's dinnertime," Uncle Andrew said. There was not a drop of anger in his voice, just a statement of fact. "The family dines together. All of us." He closed the door for her.

Anthea was halfway across the room to her trunk before she thought about it. Her guardian had ordered her to dinner, and every ounce of training told her to obey. But surely he wouldn't let her starve? If she didn't go down, someone would bring her a tray.

Then the words "The family dines together. All of us," echoed in her head. The family. No one had ever said that to her before, and it made her want to cry. Why now? Why this family? After all this time, why did it have to be this way?

〜✺〜

"Are you a great supporter of the navy?" Jillian asked as Anthea stepped into the dining room. "Or just sailors? Perhaps you are pining for some handsome young midshipman?"

Anthea stopped. She stood in the doorway, shifting from foot to foot, not sure what her cousin was talking about or where to sit. She had chosen a blue poplin dress with a white linen sailor collar. It was her second-best gown, and looked very good with her rose.

Jillian herself was wearing layer after layer of pink tulle, foaming around her like a ballerina's skirts. But instead of a blouse she wore a man's black velvet smoking jacket that had been tailored to fit her figure. Ropes of pearls filled the gap between the lapels, and more had been wound in her curly hair. She was looking at Anthea as though Anthea were the one who had dressed strangely.

"I beg your pardon?" Anthea said.

"I only wondered if you were waiting for a sailor to come home," Jillian said. She gestured at Anthea's gown, causing a large ring on her hand to flash.

"Jilly," said Uncle Andrew in a warning voice. "Be kind."

Realizing belatedly that she was being insulted, Anthea blushed. Putting her chin up she took the seat her uncle indicated and draped her napkin over her lap.

"It must be difficult, trapped up here, trying to piece something stylish together from old magazines and gossip," Anthea said coolly.

Jillian stared daggers at her, and Finn gave a low whistle before hiding his smile behind his water glass. It seemed that the "family" consisted of not only Uncle Andrew and Jillian, but also the boy Finn and Caillin MacRennie, who came stumping into the room with his graying side-whiskers bristling and a black dinner jacket that looked decidedly odd with his kilt.

There was some sort of charm dangling from his belt, Anthea noticed. It looked like a *C*, but from the way it was hanging she didn't think it was. Realizing that she was staring at the older man's kilt, she pulled her attention to the others.

Finn looked quite presentable, in a blue suit and with his blond hair brushed. He was tall and lean, his face brown from being in the sun, in contrast to his blue eyes. He caught Anthea looking at him, now, and raised his eyebrows. Anthea studied her plate.

Uncle Andrew waited until a maid had served the soup before clearing his throat to talk. He stirred his soup with a spoon, then cleared his throat again without eating and began.

"I know that you think that you're being punished, Anthea," he said. "You think that you're being sent here because no one there wants you, and this is the last place you have left before the orphanage."

Anthea opened her mouth, but then just put soup in it. That was exactly what she thought, and since Andrew seemed to be implying that this was not the case, she might as well listen.

"The truth is that I've been trying to get you back for years. Yes, *back*," he said before she could interrupt. "Caillin

MacRennie and Jilly both told me that you don't remember them, but you were born right here in this very house. It wasn't until your father died that you left, and it wasn't my wish, or the wish of anyone here, that you should leave.

"A lawyer was sent from Travertine to fetch you, and there was nothing we could do without being arrested for kidnapping. I've written to every one of your guardians over the years, begging to get you back, but all they do is move you from place to place, trying to hide you from me. It wasn't until that wife of Daniel's had her attack of the vapors that one of *them* actually contacted *me*."

Anthea's mouth was open again, this time in astonishment, a spoonful of soup forgotten halfway to her lips. She looked over and saw Jillian had much the same expression. Both girls took hasty sips of the soup and looked away from each other.

"It was your father's wish that you always remain here, in the place he loved and with the horses he loved," Uncle Andrew went on.

Anthea's heart knocked against her ribs; she felt alternately hot and cold. Her father had *loved* horses? Wrong as it sounded to her ears, it felt right in her heart.

"He suspected, as I did, that you had the Way. He had it, and so do Finn and Caillin MacRennie."

Jillian dropped her spoon, splashing soup onto her jacket. She snarled and blotted the stain with her napkin. Anthea felt her eyebrows creeping toward her hairline. If her father had

had this "Way," why didn't Andrew have it? They were brothers. And what about Jillian, who had lived with horses all her life?

"And so we come to the heart of things," Uncle Andrew said gravely. "The Way is rare, and without it we would have little to no control over the horses. We need everyone with the Way to help!"

Anthea dropped her own spoon, but for once in her life managed to avoid staining her gown. "What do you mean, you don't have control over the horses?" Her voice came out far too shrill. "Could they . . . attack?"

Did horses attack people? Like wild animals? They didn't look like wild animals, with their harnesses on and the men petting them like dogs. But she remembered the scream of the herd stallion and shivered.

"Attack?" Jillian hooted with derision. "Are we a widdle afwaid?"

"Jilly," her father said, the warning in his voice even more dire.

"I just meant—I just—" Anthea stammered. Then she put her hand to the rose at her throat and squared her shoulders. "I didn't think that the Crown had allowed you people to keep some of the horses alive."

"You people?" Jillian growled.

"*Allowed* us to keep some horses alive?" Finn said, cutting across Jillian's outrage. He clenched his jaw, and Anthea could see the muscles working there. "I can't—I just don't even know where to begin."

"Well, I mean," Anthea said hastily, "not *allowed* you to keep the horses alive, but is helping you keep them alive. What with all the diseases, and—"

"What diseases?" Jillian asked, raising one eyebrow. "Finn, are you diseased?" She turned to Anthea. "Do *I* look diseased to you?"

"Jilly," her father said again. "You know very well what she's been taught." He sighed and kneaded his forehead for a moment. "First of all, Anthea, you should know that you need have no fear of getting sick because of the horses. The rumors that horses are full of disease are not true."

"Then what killed the rest of them?" Anthea asked.

"Stop," Andrew said, when both Jilly and Finn opened their mouths. "Not now." He sighed again. "Anthea, there is so much more to the story. More than can be discussed over one dinner.

"But what you should know is that, first of all, you need have no fear that the horses will make you sick. I would not live here, with my daughter, and now my niece, if that were possible. The second thing you need to know is that the Crown does not have any idea that the Last Farm exists.

"For all the king and his people know, every horse died centuries past, along with anyone who had the Way. And it's because they teach that horses cause diseases and plague that we must keep ourselves secret, to protect our charges."

"How do you keep a place secret that is so big and so filled with enormous animals?" Anthea blurted out.

"Who's going to tattle on us to the southerners?" Jillian said. "You?"

"Jilly," Uncle Andrew said.

"Well, is she?" Finn demanded.

"How dare you?"

Anthea's outrage came out as a question, because she didn't know what she was really saying. How dare he imply that she was a tattletale? Or how dare he think that . . . what . . . she would tell the Crown they had horses? Was it illegal to have horses? They were still under the sovereignty of the Crown, but did that mean that . . . ? She couldn't think what it meant.

"The land here, north of the Wall, is ignored by the Crown," Uncle Andrew said. "I don't even think they realized that there was such a large, prominent estate here when they built the Wall. The main part of this very house is older than the Royal Palace at Travertine."

Anthea was about to protest, but looking up at the age-blackened beams of the tall ceiling, she believed it.

"This has been our family's great work, since the Wall was built," her uncle went on. "It was your father's entire life: keeping the horses safe, training them, finding those who had the Way and bringing them here. This was what he did."

"What? No!" Anthea stood up. Then, not knowing where to go or what to do, she sat down.

"It's another long story," Uncle Andrew said. "One I would be much happier to tell you, but I can see you already have a lot to sort out first.

"As for being able to control them, well, the horses are like no other animal you've encountered. They are far more intelligent, for one thing. They cannot be ordered about, they must be worked with carefully. The Way will allow you to work with them more effectively. They will respect you, and listen to you, more than a rider who does not have the Way.

"We need you, Anthea. It's what your father would have wanted."

Anthea ignored the prickle of guilt that came with the mention of her father.

"I'm glad you are trying to honor my father's wishes," she said, very politely, and as a way of covering up the turmoil in her brain. "But a girl belongs to her mother, and it's clear from my mother's will that she wanted me to be raised far from here." She took a sip of water, and looked up to find everyone staring at her.

"Her will?" Uncle Andrew blinked. "What will? What have they told you about her?"

Anthea put down her glass, feeling the water and soup churn in her stomach. "What *should* they have told me about her?" Her voice trembled.

Jillian opened her mouth, but her father shot her a look and she subsided, her eyes wide.

"My dear Anthea," Andrew said gently, "your mother is very much alive!"

Florian

Florian had waited as patiently as he was able for Beloved Anthea to come to him, and still she had not appeared. The Thornley had been keeping her from him; Florian knew it to be true. The Thornley assigned horses to riders; he should have brought Beloved Anthea to Florian at once. Yet she did not leave the Big House with the other human foals each day. They came in their herd: She Who Was Jilly, the Soon King, That Leggy Boy . . . but not Beloved Anthea.

What task had The Thornley given to Beloved Anthea that she spent her days in the Big House? Why were they being kept apart in this way?

He stood in his paddock and cried out to her, but she would not look at him. He cried out to her until one of the men came, thinking that Florian was ill. Florian moved away from the man, irritated. The wind brought him Beloved Anthea's scent, and it was not well. It was filled with fear and anger, and he longed to go to her.

The man tried to move Florian to a far paddock, one where he could not see her window. Florian screamed with rage, and now two men came and tried to draw him away. He kicked and bit, knowing that it was bad of him, but not caring.

Florian was so filled with emotion that he hardly knew what he was doing. He ramped and reared, kicking and trumpeting his displeasure. Three men, now, were trying to calm him, to tie a rope to his halter and lead him away. He didn't want to go away, he wanted to go to his Beloved.

The High One's voice cut across the voices of the men. The High One, called Constantine by the men, had seen Florian's shameful rage and demanded that Florian calm himself.

With the greatest of efforts, Florian brought all four hooves to the ground. He lowered his head, bowing in shame in the direction of the High One, who glared from his private paddock. Florian trembled, and almost wished that there were not two fences separating them. He wished that the High One were there to bite him, to kick . . . to make him feel anything but this loss over seeing Beloved Anthea so close and yet still cut off from him.

One of the grooms threw a scarf over Florian's head to darken his eyes and muffle his ears—almost as great a shame as being reprimanded by the High One, yet the men thought it was soothing—and Florian meekly allowed them to lead him away.

Beloved Anthea would come to him, and Florian's anger would be gone. But she did not, and he began to lose hope. And then he began to grow angry again.

THE LETTER

Dear Aunt Deirdre,

    I thank you from the bottom of my heart for the beautiful silver rose you sent me. It was certainly a bright spot on a dark day. I will wear it always, as a reminder both of your regard and of what I strive to be.

    Nothing here beyond the Wall is as I was led to believe. I do not wish to cause you any trauma in your delicate condition, but I am eager for your advice. A young lady, such as myself, alone in such a place, has no example upon which to rely but those she has left behind.

    It seems that horses still exist.

    According to my uncle Andrew Thornley, horses

were not the cause of the plague all those years ago,
and so he has devoted his life (and claims that my
father also devoted his) to preserving the species.
They call this estate the Last Farm, and say that it
lies in Leana, which is apparently a real place and not
a myth. Last Farm is home to dozens of horses, as
well as people who claim to have something called the
Way, which allows them to communicate with the
beasts.

Andrew Thornley is insisting that I be educated
about the creatures here, and associate not just with
the handlers but with the beasts as well. I am not
sure what to do.

I have also been told a vicious rumor, one
that my hand shakes to report. (Please excuse my
handwriting.) Andrew Thornley claims that my
mother lives. I do not know what purpose it serves
him to tell me this, but I cannot believe it to be true.
Do you know of any reason why he would think to tell
me such a lie?

Your devoted niece,
Anthea

Anthea set down her pen and carefully read through her
letter. And again. She stared out the window at the bustling
farm. A week had gone by since that first wretched dinner. Her
uncle claimed her mother hadn't died, nor had she abandoned

Anthea. Her uncle claimed that her mother was simply busy with her work. Anthea had nodded politely and then retreated to her room.

Her uncle Andrew was lying.

How could any Rose Matron of Coronam be too busy to see her own daughter? Not only that, but genteel matrons, even those who were not former Rose Maidens, did not work! *Anthea* was supposed to be her mother's work. She could not understand why her uncle would say something so cruel to her.

Anthea had paced her room for days, trying to figure out what was real and what was lies. Trying to decide whom to turn to for help. In the end she had decided on Aunt Deirdre. Even though she knew that her aunt was the reason why she had been sent here, Anthea could not help but think that a Rose Maiden, like her mother, would be the best person to give advice to a young lady. Also, the gift of the silver rose Anthea wore constantly seemed to indicate either some hidden fondness—or at worst a sense of guilt.

Either way, Anthea had decided to appeal to her aunt rather than her uncle. It still took her two days to compose the letter, and another day to get up the courage to send it. She finally sealed the letter and put it on her breakfast tray with a note begging the maid to post it for her.

As soon as she had sent it, Anthea was even more upset than she had been before. What if all the secrecy about Last Farm wasn't just hysteria? What if Aunt Deirdre told . . . someone . . . and they told the king and he became angry about the horses? Anthea asked the maid later if she had posted the letter, hoping she could take it back, but it was already gone.

"Best to forget it then," Anthea told herself. "Besides which, if Aunt Deirdre believes me, and if she tells someone, whom would she tell? And would they believe her?"

Her aunt was a Rose Matron, but in her condition she was hardly hosting a ball every night. And Anthea had always suspected that her aunt had not been as highly favored a Maiden as her mother was . . . *is?*

It was just too much.

Anthea would have stayed in her room forever if Jillian hadn't knocked on her door, loudly and long, that very morning. Anthea had just been writing the greeting to her aunt, and she hurried to hide the letter under the blotter before unlocking her door. When she at last answered, her cousin curtly informed her that she needed to be upstairs in the schoolroom for lessons in half an hour.

"What kind of lessons?" Anthea had asked with trepidation.

"Oh, I'm sorry," Jilly said with exaggerated concern. "Do Rose Maidens not know arithmetic? Are they forbidden from reading literature?"

"You mean *lesson* lessons?" Anthea said, incredulous that these people valued anything beyond their disgraceful horses.

Jillian rolled her eyes and closed the door.

Anthea stumbled into one of her school uniforms and splashed water on her face. As much as she hurried, there was no sign of Jillian when she emerged from her room, and so

Anthea set off to find the schoolroom alone. After wandering the halls of the sprawling house for several minutes, she ran into a gangly boy carrying a stack of books.

"Oh, it's you," he'd said, a suspicious look on his dark face.

"Please take me to the schoolroom," Anthea said.

He led her there without comment and without introducing himself, though he obviously knew who she was. Once in the schoolroom, a bright, airy space with rows of windows that occupied the top of the east wing, Anthea found herself greeted warmly by a beautiful woman in an elegant shirtwaist. Miss Ravel was the farm's schoolteacher, and Anthea soon found that not only was she from Travertine, but had also attended Miss Miniver's Rose Academy.

"You poor thing," Miss Ravel said as she shook Anthea's hand. "You have had a very trying few days, I am sure."

She pointed Anthea to a desk, unfortunately between Finn and Jillian, who both ignored her—though Jillian did mutter something about hoisting a mainsail when she saw Anthea's clothes. Miss Ravel gave Anthea some books and started the handful of younger children, all boys, on their lessons, before starting the older ones, which included Anthea, Jillian, Finn, and the other boy, whose name was Keth, on arithmetic.

It was all so familiar and soothing that Anthea felt tears prickling her eyes. She looked up at Miss Ravel's smiling face and thought, too, that here was an ally. When lessons were over at lunchtime, Anthea waited behind to speak to Miss Ravel privately.

But as Finn went out, Miss Ravel called gaily to him.

"Oh, Finn! When you go to the stables, tell my dear Daffodil I will be out to ride her as soon as I mark these papers!"

Finn nodded and smiled, and then shot Anthea a pointed look, as though making sure that she heard what Miss Ravel had said.

Anthea had most definitely heard. Every word fell into her like a rock. Miss Ravel was one of *them*. These horse worshippers. She wasn't going to give Anthea permission to stay away from the stables, as her next words confirmed.

"What is it, dear? You best hurry so that you can eat a good lunch. I understand that today is to be your first riding lesson!" Miss Ravel had beamed as though Anthea were about to enjoy a special treat.

"Nothing, miss," Anthea said in a hoarse whisper. "I forgot."

Anthea fled from the schoolroom for the safety of her bedroom. She could not and *would not* ride a horse! She locked the door behind her for good measure.

It wasn't long before she heard another loud knock. "Go away, Jillian! I want to be alone!"

"Anthea, I need to speak with you," Uncle Andrew's voice boomed through the door. Anthea's hands started shaking.

"No thank you, Uncle," she said as calmly as she could manage.

She heard a jingling and then a clicking, and Uncle Andrew

walked into the room. He held up a key, his expression sheepish.

"I didn't mean to scare you, but I knew you would never let me in."

"You have a key to my room?" she said in horror.

"I wouldn't have used it unless it was important," Uncle Andrew said.

"Is it important?" Anthea's voice sounded shrill, and she winced.

"It is," he said gently. "Anthea, we need to talk."

"I think you've said enough," Anthea said.

She winced again, saying it. It was something she had once heard Miss Miniver say to a man who had gotten fresh with her at an outing to the Travertine Rose Gardens. Anthea had always longed to use it, but saying it now made her feel deeply stupid. Also, it didn't really fit. Her uncle *hadn't* said enough: she still had far too many questions.

"I am sorry that we dropped the load of bricks on your head that first night," Uncle Andrew told her. "It had honestly never occurred to me that you would be told your mother was dead. I wasn't sure if you had ever had contact with her, but . . . dead? I'm so sorry. It just sort of burst out of me, I was so surprised."

"I, um, thank you for the apology," Anthea said.

"I'm sure you're wondering why they told you she was dead," Uncle Andrew said.

Something had occurred to Anthea. She looked at her uncle and said, to his evident surprise, "I don't think anyone ever did."

Over the past few days she had been thinking back on anything that she had ever heard about her parents, her mother especially, trying to piece together any hints that her mother might have been alive. It now came to her that no one had ever told her that her mother had died.

"They said my father had died," Anthea said. "They said he was with my mother, at the seaside on holiday." She looked up at Andrew, dazed. "Then they said that I had to go live with an aunt. They said my father provided handsomely for me. No one ever says your mother left you an inheritance, because her property belonged to my father."

Uncle Andrew nodded.

"They just never talked about her at all."

"No, they wouldn't have," Andrew said. "You see, she is a very unusual woman, your mother, and—"

"You have to promise me something," Anthea said suddenly, interrupting him.

"Yes?"

"You have to promise that you will never lie to me."

"I'm sorry that others have lied to you, I want you to know that—"

"It's not that they have," Anthea said. "It's that they . . . never told me the truth. They never really told me anything."

"But I do want to tell you," Uncle Andrew said.

"I can see that. So, can I trust that all these things that you're telling me are true?"

"Yes, Anthea," he said, very seriously. "I swear it. I could never lie to you. I loved your father, my brother, very dearly. I would not lie to his daughter."

"I think that's all I can talk about right now," she said.

"Fair enough," Uncle Andrew said. "I wanted you to have some time to think."

"Thank you."

"But now, I'm afraid, that time is over," he continued briskly. "I've told Cassie no more trays. We need you, Anthea. It's time for you to take up your birthright, and get on a horse."

Her uncle stepped out into the hallway and then returned with a bundle of clothes and a pair of boots.

"These are Jilly's," he explained. "But they should fit you well enough. She says your feet are the same size, and well, you're only a little taller."

He put the boots down, and handed Anthea the clothes. To her dismay, it looked like the topmost garment was a pair of the tight-fitting trousers she had seen Jilly wearing to ride in. They would not be as tight on Anthea, but still—they were *trousers*.

"I'm very sorry, but we've given you nearly a week to think things over. It's time, Anthea. You can have the afternoon to get used to the idea, but tomorrow after breakfast I'll take you down to the stables to meet the horse you'll be riding.

"Her name is Bluebell."

8

ONCE WAS LOST

IN THE WATERY MORNING sunlight, Anthea studied the pile of clothes on her bed. She had picked them out the night before, but they still looked strange.

There was a man's tweed jacket, taken in at the shoulders and waist for a girl. A plain white linen blouse. And the trousers, made of thick serge, but lined with a silky material that felt far too exotic for comfort. She began to pace.

She had tossed and turned all night—yet another sleepless night in this place. She couldn't get on a horse! She couldn't even bring herself to try on the trousers. They were revealing and strange and mannish and awful! She had never even worn pajamas: nightgowns were far more ladylike and proper. What if Finn or one of the other young men saw her?

Anthea looked at the clock. She had less than ten minutes before her uncle came to fetch her.

"I can't! I just can't!" Anthea burst out.

She ran to the door, then checked herself. She listened for a moment, then carefully opened it and peered down the hall in both directions. It appeared that everyone was already at breakfast. Anthea tiptoed down the hall toward the back of the house. She had no idea where she was going, but surely if everyone was in the great hall, there would be plenty of places to hide.

Just for one more day, she told herself. Just . . . until she got used to the idea of the trousers. Or perhaps she could appeal to her uncle to let her ride in a skirt. Jillian surely didn't want to share her wardrobe with Anthea. Perhaps Anthea could ask her for help in finding something more ladylike. That would buy Anthea time.

Anthea found a small staircase at the end of the hallway, and went down rather than up, knowing that up would lead to the schoolroom. At the bottom of the stairs she ducked down a narrow corridor that went off at an angle from the main house. She listened at a keyhole before opening the door when she heard someone coming out of a room behind her.

Quick as a flash she was turning the heavy, old-fashioned latch, and then she was through and closing the door behind her. She blinked, the light suddenly bright in her eyes, and gasped as she realized that she was outside.

It was the first time she had set a foot outside since the day she had slogged through the mud to tell her uncle she wanted no part of this. Since she had saved a horse from choking. Since she had found out she had the Way.

Now here she was on the edge of the open area in front of the house, standing at the end of one of the sprawling wings. There was a neatly raked stretch of gravel, and then the huge sprawling building they called the stables.

She had seen horses going in and out of it from her window, and guessed that that was where they slept. But the doors were open now, and all the horses were off in the fields, and the men with them. No one was around to see her. She walked straight toward the stables, her heart pounding. They would never suspect her of hiding there!

She took a deep breath and held it as she walked into the dimly lit building, not sure what to expect. There were lanterns hanging on each side of a wide central aisle, and stalls with low doors, not unlike any barn where oxen or cattle were kept. When she finally took a breath, she found that the smell was actually tolerable.

She had a rush of memory, something about jumping into a pile of hay, of having a horse rub its nose on her face, but she fought it down. She grabbed an empty metal bucket from the corner and started down the aisle to one of the stalls about midway along. Checking carefully to make sure the straw inside was fresh—it was—she went into the stall and turned the bucket over to sit on.

"There," she said aloud, with a sigh of relief.

Anthea wished that she had brought something to read. Or some paper and a pencil. Anything to distract her from thoughts of riding horses, and the news of her not-at-all-deceased mother.

Since she had nothing to write with, she tried to compose a letter to her mother in her head. What would one even say to one's long-lost mother after so many years?

"Hello, why did you leave me?" Anthea said aloud.

There was a thud from the stall next to hers. The wooden wall shook. Anthea's heart stuttered and she clapped a hand to her mouth. She waited, but heard nothing.

"He-hello?" she called out at last.

Another thud.

"Who's there?"

There was a massive thud and a splintering sound.

Anthea stood up, afraid of what she might find on the other side of the wall. She peeked over the half door of the stall she was in. There was no one she could see in the wide corridor, or any of the stalls across the way.

Thud. Splinter.

A wave of emotion.

It wasn't a person in the stall next to hers; it was a horse, Anthea realized with relief. Her hiding place was secure, for now. Although if the silly beast didn't stop that racket, some-one would surely come to see what was wrong, and find Anthea.

"*Shh,*" she said loudly. "Shush, you!"

The thudding stopped, but Anthea still didn't sit back

down on her bucket. Waves of longing crashed over her. Longing. Sorrow. And the deepest love.

Anthea stood in the straw, her head cocked to one side. She felt like she was hearing music in another room, a tune that she knew but couldn't quite name.

Beloved.

"Oh," Anthea whispered, and tears began to fall gently from her eyes.

FLORIAN

At last.

At last.

Beloved Anthea had come to him at last! Florian could hardly contain his joy when she opened the door of his stall. They gazed at each other for a long time.

"It's you," she said.

He lifted his head and breathed gently into her face. There were tears on her cheeks. He blotted them dry with his nose, then put his head over her shoulder. She wrapped her arms around his neck and laid her cheek alongside his.

"It's you," she whispered.

Here I am, Beloved, Florian thought. *Here you are. At last.*

"At last."

9

Now Is Found

THE HORSE WAS BEAUTIFUL. Anthea had little basis for comparison, but all the same . . . this was the most beautiful horse in the world. His legs were long and strong, and he had smooth muscles under his glowing golden-brown hide. His thick mane and tail were black, and so were the tall stockings on his legs, and the velvety end of his nose.

"Beautiful," Anthea told him as she continued to hold and stroke him.

And as she held him, memories came flooding back. Memories of a tall handsome man with dark hair, like Uncle Andrew, but not. Her father, whose face she had almost forgotten until she saw his brother.

Memories of drawing horses, of talking about horses with Jilly. Memories of wearing a charm like Caillin MacRennie's, shaped like what she now realized was a horseshoe and hung on braided horsehair. Even now she could feel it scratching her neck, though she didn't know where it had gone.

Memories that explained the dream.

All her life she had dreamed of flying. Skimming above the ground with her arms outstretched and a man's voice laughing in her ear. Now it unfolded in her mind, and she knew: that man was her father, and they weren't flying, they were riding a horse. In the dream her eyes were watering from the stinging wind of their flight, which prevented her from seeing their surroundings.

Was it this horse they had ridden? She looked at him intently.

He looked back with dark intelligent eyes. She had seen him in the paddocks, she felt sure, but the only horse she could recognize was the screaming Constantine, who was more reddish, with a black shawl-like marking on his shoulders.

This horse, this beautiful, gentle horse pulled back and regarded her for a moment, then he sighed so deeply that the gust of breath plastered Anthea's blouse to her chest. She giggled as her lace-trimmed collar tickled her neck. The horse leaned forward and put his nose on her shoulder, snuffling.

Through the Way, Anthea caught a strange stirring from him, a welter of impressions that involved a man's voice, the taste of sugar, being warm . . . and then being cold and the voice stopping, the sugar going away. The horse smelled her deeply and then he leaned his head against her shoulder, sighing again. A sense of coming home washed through Anthea, and she put her arms around the horse's head again and held him tightly.

"My darling," she murmured. "My precious boy. I'm sorry you were alone."

The sound of voices and boots clomping on the stable floor disturbed Anthea's reverie. The horse snorted, bothered as well, but neither he nor Anthea moved.

From outside the stall she heard Jillian and Finn talking. Keth added something, and Anthea's cousin laughed loudly as they came down the aisle.

"Wherever Her Majesty is hiding," Jillian said, "you have to admire her. We live here, and we can't find her."

Anthea would have been offended, but all she could think about was this horse and how wonderful it was to simply stand here with him, breathing in unison.

"Be kind," Finn said.

"Oh, I'm so sorry!" Jillian said with exaggerated concern. "Was I not being gracious about Her Majesty?"

"Just . . . be kind, Jilly," Finn said.

There was a splash and a smacking noise. A strangled cry. Jillian and Keth laughed. Then another splash and a splat, and Jillian screamed with indignation.

"You—you—you!" she spluttered.

"Be kind!" Finn said, but he was laughing now, and the door of a stall banged shut. There was another splat and a whoop from Keth.

The horse stamped a foot, and irritation flashed through his emotions. Anthea agreed, and stamped one of her feet as well. The horse laid back his ears and made a grumbling sound. If she could have made such a noise, Anthea would have.

"*Shh, shh*, you'll make him mad," Jillian said, but she was giggling.

"They're all out in the paddocks," Keth said, dismissive.

"Except for the troublemaker," Jillian said. "The horse equivalent of our friend Finn," she teased.

Another splat.

"You brat! Would you throw a wet sponge at Her Majesty, Miss Anthea?" Jillian demanded. "Or do you think she's too fine? Too byoo-tee-full?"

A splat and a squawk.

"I'll get you for that!" Jillian declared.

There was a clatter of boots coming down the aisle. The boots skidded to a stop right outside the stall where Anthea was standing, meditatively stroking the neck of the horse.

"What in the—" Finn said. "Jilly, quick!"

"Oh no, I'm not falling for that," Jillian called from farther down the stable.

"Jilly! Go get your father!"

"Wait, are you serious?" Keth's voice came closer. "What is—" He broke off with a gasp.

"Don't move, Anthea," Finn instructed. "Keth, go get Captain Thornley. Now!"

Anthea wasn't planning on moving. She was enjoying

feeling the smooth hide of the horse, and running her fingers through his long silky mane. She was irritated with Finn for bothering them.

Finally Jillian came to the door of the stall. She gasped and whispered to Finn for a moment before talking to Anthea.

"Are you all right?" Jillian asked in a low voice.

"Yes," Anthea said.

She felt at ease for the first time in days. She wrapped her left arm around the horse's neck and rubbed between his ears with her right. He drooped against her with pleasure, and she had to widen her stance to keep him from knocking her over.

"We're fine."

Naturally they were fine. Together, they would always be fine.

"That's *Florian*," Jillian said in a choked voice.

"Oh," Anthea said. "Florian!"

He made a chuckling noise. Anthea was embarrassed that she had forgotten, but now that she heard the name, she felt like she had always known it.

"Didn't my father warn you?" Jillian whispered.

Anthea shook her head, and so did the horse. Florian. Why would she need to be warned about Florian? She continued to stroke his ears.

"Anthea," Jillian whispered, "what were you doing in here?"

"I hid in here," Anthea said simply. "Because I don't want

to learn to ride." She hurried to reassure Florian. "Except for you! I wasn't hiding from *you*."

"Oh no no no!" Jillian babbled. "Finn, what are we going to do? I think she's gone mad!"

"She has not gone mad," Finn said. "Keep your voice down."

"Then what's wrong with her?" Jillian demanded in a loud whisper. "Anthea?" she called softly. "I'm sorry I made fun of your clothes. And called you Your Majesty just now." There was a faint creak as she lifted the latch of the stall door. "Now please come out of there. Slowly."

"I can't leave him," Anthea said, and her voice broke a little. "I left him before, you see."

"Oh," Jillian said, and she sounded like there was something in her throat.

"How could I have forgotten him?" Anthea said. She leaned back so that she could look deeply into Florian's eyes. "How could I have forgotten you?" she asked.

Waves of love came from the horse. She knew that he didn't blame her. She apologized to him all the same.

"That's wonderful," Jillian whispered. "So wonderful! But I want you to let go of the horse now, Anthea, and step back."

"Jillian Thornley! You aren't teasing that poor beast, are you?"

Caillin MacRennie's voice intruded before Anthea could sink back into her reverie. It was just so warm and nice here in Florian's stall.

"I would never!" Jillian was indignant. "Anthea went into *Florian's* stall. She doesn't know he's been acting up." Her voice was full of concern.

"Jillian cares about me," Anthea murmured to Florian. "And I care about her. But I *love* you."

"Ah, so you found him," Caillin MacRennie said, his gruff voice almost tender. "Now, Florian, ye can stop bein' such a terror. There's your girl back."

"His girl?" Anthea freed herself and looked over the stall door at the old man.

"Florian was the last of your father's horses," Caillin Mac-Rennie said. "And your first. Delivered the wee foal himself, with you assistin'. Raised him up by hand, you did, giving Florian sugar and carrots and once a whole pie that you stole from the kitchen. He used to chase you and your papa, when he'd ride you over the hills on Justinian."

Anthea reached out again and laid her hand flat between Florian's eyes. "We used to go flying over the hills together. With Papa."

Feelings of warmth and security overwhelmed Anthea as the tears rolled down her cheeks.

She had found Florian. He had found her.

"It's you at last," she whispered.

FLORIAN

Beloved Anthea had come to him at last. Florian felt his heart straining to contain his joy. Beloved Anthea rubbed his ears in just the way he had always liked, and he breathed in her scent.

All the noise and fury, the storm of emotions that he had experienced over the past weeks faded away. Nothing else mattered, but that Beloved Anthea was here at last. With him.

They must never be parted again.

10

Dinner with a King

"it's out of the question," Uncle Andrew said again.

"But he needs me," Anthea wheedled.

"Florian's turned round again. Taken to her like the missing piece o' himself," Caillin MacRennie put in from his end of the dinner table, and Anthea gave him a grateful look.

"Well, that goes without saying," Uncle Andrew said. "Charles always wanted . . ." He stopped and cleared his throat.

"You may care for him, of course," he said, after a minute. "Keep his stall clean, make sure he's fed. Jilly will teach you how, and how to groom him. But there will be no riding stallions, young lady!"

Anthea never thought she would feel this way, but she was decidedly put out at her uncle's refusal to let her ride Florian.

Uncle Andrew wanted her to learn to ride, and she had apologized for hiding from him, and had shaken hands in a very adult way. Then she had proposed that they compromise by having her learn to ride on Florian. Somehow, touching a horse didn't seem so horrible, if it was Florian.

But Uncle Andrew was being completely unreasonable. How could he claim he was delighted that she had found Florian, yet not let her ride him? How could he applaud her mature decision to stop hiding and take riding lessons and then tell her that the very reason for her willingness was unacceptable?

"Not even Jilly rides stallions," Finn said.

Anthea snorted. Everyone stared at her. Jillian made an indignant noise.

"I—I am sorry," Anthea said. "I didn't mean—"

"You think because I don't have the Way—" Jillian began.

"What?" Anthea looked at her cousin in growing horror. "I didn't mean . . . I just meant . . . Florian and I have a special bond. If you had a bond with a stallion . . . do you have a bond with a stallion?"

Anthea closed her mouth before she could continue to babble. It was only a few hours since she and Jillian had made peace, and now Anthea had ruined it with her pleading to ride Florian.

"No, I don't," Jillian said stiffly.

"Jilly, you know what she means," Finn said. He frowned at Uncle Andrew. "Don't you think, in light of the situation . . . ?" he asked enigmatically.

"No, I don't," Andrew said.

"But, sir," Finn said, raising his eyebrows.

"Finn," Andrew said, lowering his.

Anthea and Jillian watched the two talking as if it were a tennis match. Anthea had never heard a young man challenge his elder like this. Nor had she ever seen a mature man give so much weight to a few words by a boy. She would have to ask Jillian later why Finn was allowed to speak to Uncle Andrew this way.

"She hasn't sat on a horse since she was four," Uncle Andrew said to Finn.

"That's true," Finn said thoughtfully.

"I beg your pardon, Uncle Andrew," Anthea said. He looked at her, somewhat quizzical. "But I happen to be sitting *right here.*"

"I know you are," Uncle Andrew said. "And I'm sorry to be talking over you, but this is a serious matter."

"Am I not a serious person?"

"Yes, but you see, Finn and I—"

"I'm so sorry, Uncle Andrew, but I really do find it very odd that you allow Finn to make decisions about my life, but will not listen to me."

Finn looked down at his plate. He took his fork and started to draw lines on the tablecloth with it. Anthea felt a little bad for hurting his feelings, but really, who was he to decide what horse she could ride?

"Finn is a magTaran," Jilly said.

Anthea just looked at her in confusion.

"A magTaran," Jilly said again, with greater emphasis. "King Taran—"

Uncle Andrew held up a hand to stop his daughter. "Well, there's really no other way to say this, and he's too modest to do it himself," he rambled. "So I'll just go for it. Finn is the king."

Anthea burst out laughing.

Finn's face slowly turned red, but he kept on making lines on the tablecloth.

"I'm sorry," Anthea said, and gasped, her mirth subsiding when no one else joined her. "But . . . the king of *what*?"

Jillian dropped her fork with a clatter. Uncle Andrew put his down more deliberately.

"The king of Leana," Uncle Andrew said.

Now it was Anthea's turn to drop her fork. Finn continued to study the table, while Caillin MacRennie kept on eating as though Andrew Thornley had not just calmly spoken treason over the dinner table.

"There is no king but King Gareth of Coronam," Anthea said.

Jilly snorted. "Does Kronenhof not exist then? Radij? Tendu?" She plucked at her sleeve. She was wearing a green silk Tenduhai robe and trousers tonight. Anthea didn't think her cousin actually owned a skirt, the layers of transparent tulle she draped herself with not being actual clothing.

"I mean there can't be another king in Coronam," Anthea said, trying to sound reasonable and not lose her temper with Jillian. "Leana *is* Coronam. You might as well say that I'm the queen of Bellair or Keth is the king of Travertine." She stopped to breathe a little. "And saying that he's the *rightful* king . . . where does that put King Gareth? Do you understand what you just said?" she asked Uncle Andrew directly.

"Saying Finn is the king of Leana," Caillin MacRennie said. He calmly took another bite of potato. "Is not the same as calling Keth the king of anything." Caillin MacRennie pointed one finger in the air, and then dropped it down to point at the floor once he had Anthea's attention. "*This* is Leana. The country you're standing on. The one that was, before the Coronami came."

Now Anthea, who had just picked up her fork, dropped it again. She sucked in a breath and looked at Caillin MacRennie, and then at her uncle, waiting for him to say something. And then at Finn, who surely wouldn't allow his name to be used in such a way. But all three of them were eating as though treason were not being committed over their plates of fish.

Well, Finn, in his defense, was not so much eating as now toying with his fork and a chunk of potato. She could tell that Andrew was watching her out of the corner of his eye, to gauge her reaction. Jillian was watching her with open honesty, waiting for Anthea to reply. Instead she stood up.

"This is treason," she said with a shaking voice.

"Anthea," Uncle Andrew said. "Anthea, sit down."

"No!"

"It's fine," Finn mumbled.

"It is not fine!" she stormed.

"It's not treason," Caillin MacRennie said. "It's plain truth. If the Coronami hadn't come with their army, young Finn would be the king of Leana."

Anthea felt much as she had when Uncle Andrew had told her that her mother was still alive. How many more perfectly good dinners were going to be ruined by the disclosure of shocking information? She waited a moment, wondering if this at least was some sort of test of her patriotism. But everyone was just looking at her.

"Finn should be the king?" she said at last, tentatively.

"Yes," Uncle Andrew answered her.

"Of Leana?"

"Yes."

"You're saying there was something here before . . . Coronam . . . ?"

"Yes."

Anthea could not comprehend any of this. But for Florian's sake she was going to try.

If Finn was the king, that meant that there had been a country—Leana—before Coronam. Instead of a wilderness with a few people in huts, no government, and horses running wild everywhere bringing disease and death. The Crown had to

take over this land because the horses were so dangerous—
the Crown *saved* those people from ruin and showed them a
better way to live, with brave princes leading the people, their
Rose Maiden wives and sisters supporting them.

But not one of Anthea's history books, not one of her teach-
ers or relations, ever mentioned that the people of Leana had
their own king. That they had a Way that allowed them to
communicate with horses. Or that the horses were actually
beautiful, soulful creatures. No one had ever told her that a
horse could be as wonderful as Florian.

It made her head ache to think of it.

"I want to ride Florian," was all she said.

"All right," her uncle said, much to the shock of everyone,
and not just Anthea. He held up one finger. "But first, you have
to learn *how* to ride. Children learning their alphabet are not
asked to write a poem in praise of the king right off, unless
things are vastly different at Rose Academies today?"

Anthea shook her head.

"So, you are going to learn to ride a very nice mare named
Bluebell, and then, when you have shown that you can ride Bluebell with as much skill as Jilly can ride Buttercup, we will talk
about Florian."

"If she gets to ride Florian, I get to ride Caesar," Jilly
put in.

Her father gave her a dire look. "If I see you go near Caesar, you won't back a horse for a month," he said.

"Yes, Father," Jilly said, with obviously false meekness.

"Very well," Uncle Andrew said. "Let's all get some rest. Anthea, I'm sure you have a lot to think about."

"I do," she admitted, dropping her napkin and moving away from the table.

"Meet me at the stables after breakfast," Uncle Andrew said. "I'll have you excused from morning lessons tomorrow. I want to get you started on your riding and other horse duties. Before you try to slip away again."

Anthea nodded, then walked out carefully, doing her best not to jostle her head, which felt entirely too full.

11

BRIDLES, BLUEBELL, AND BRUISES

"THIS IS BLUEBELL." Uncle Andrew took the reins of a dappled gray horse from one of the grooms, and the man grinned at Anthea as he ducked out of the paddock.

Anthea was glad to see him go. She wanted as few people as possible to watch her first riding lesson. She knew that she was going to humiliate herself somehow, and the fewer people who saw, the better. Once the groom was gone she returned her attention to Uncle Andrew, who was waiting patiently alongside Bluebell.

"Bluebell will be your responsibility from now on," Uncle Andrew informed her. "You will ride her, groom her, clean her stall and tack."

"Tack?"

"Saddle, bridle, et cetera. If you have questions, Jilly or Keth can advise you, but you need to do the work yourself. If I find out you've neglected any of these chores . . ."

She gave him a sly look. "You'll send me to my room?"

"No, I'll make you muck the manure out of all the stalls for a week," he shot back. "It's the standard penalty for anyone who neglects their duties."

Anthea shuddered.

"Exactly," her uncle said. "But for now, let's just get you up on her back, and teach you how to sit."

"Teach me how to sit?" Anthea eyed the horse. She could just see over her back, and her head was even higher. "Are you sure you want me riding one this big?"

She fluttered her fingers at one of the far paddocks that held some horses that looked much less menacing from this distance. Their brown and black hides looked solid and reassuring, whereas Bluebell was thundercloud gray, her mane and tail a mix of dirty white and black that made her look even more stormy.

"That's Leonidas, Domitian, and Theodorus," Uncle Andrew said as though their names explained everything.

Anthea merely blinked at him.

"They're stallions," he clarified. "All the stallions are named after kings and warriors from old legends: Constantine, Gaius Julius, Marcus Antonius. They're all battle trained.

"The mares are not trained to fight. They're named for flowers: Bluebell, Blossom, Daffodil, Marigold, Campanula. Jilly's horse is Buttercup."

Anthea was offended. Did the mares *have* to have such silly names? *Buttercup*? And "Campanula" sounded like a skin disease. But the stallions were all given noble appellations *and* trained to battle? She couldn't see any difference between Bluebell and the three in the other paddock, except for the color. But she bit back an acid remark since she supposed it really was better if she stayed away from the stallions. Except for Florian. Was Florian trained to fight?

Before she could ask, Uncle Andrew arranged the reins on the horse's neck and then laced his fingers together, holding out his cupped palms to her. "Put your knee in," he said.

"Beg pardon?"

"Your knee. The left one. Put it in my hands, and I'll boost you up."

Anthea hesitated. She'd seen some of the men mounting their horses from her window, but they usually just gave a jump and a sort of swing and were up. She'd seen Jillian in the saddle, too, but never noticed how she got there. How could her uncle holding her knee get her in the saddle?

Bluebell shifted and sighed, and Anthea caught a thought from her. Something about hay, and a feeling of boredom. She was boring the *horse*? Bad enough that Anthea had her uncle and the rest of the brigade to judge her, but the horses as well? That was too much!

She put her knee into Uncle Andrew's cupped hands and he heaved her into the air. She screeched and leaped backward out of his hands, barely managing to land on her feet.

"Sorry, should have explained more," her uncle said, giving Bluebell a comforting rub on the neck. "Now, grab hold of the pommel with your left hand—that's the front of the saddle. Good. Now hold the cantle—that's the back—with your right. When I lift, move your right hand and swing your right leg over."

"Oh. I see." She nodded sagely even though she didn't understand any of it.

"Let's try it again."

He cupped his hands and she put her knee into them, grabbing the saddle at the same time. Her uncle heaved, she pulled, the horse's ears went back, and she was suddenly hanging from the saddle with her legs held stiffly above the ground by her uncle.

"Pull yourself up," he grunted, raising her a little more.

"I'm trying!"

The next thing Anthea knew, her uncle had both his hands under her buttocks and was shoving her into the saddle. She pulled herself up as hard as she could, kicking her feet like a swimmer, until she was lying across Bluebell's back. Then Uncle Andrew took hold of her right leg and threw it up and over the horse's rump, and she was sitting upright.

"Oh," was all she could say as waves of heat pulsed in her cheeks and she prayed that no one else had been watching. "So that's why I'm wearing trousers."

Jillian had flatly refused to help Anthea find a dress or skirt to ride in. Instead she had shaken her curls and told Anthea to wait and see. Anthea had compromised by wearing the trousers and boots with her own school uniform blouse, instead of one of Jilly's men's jackets.

"Put your feet in the stirrups," Uncle Andrew said calmly.

She fumbled her feet into the metal things hanging from each side of the saddle, and then fumbled with the reins as her uncle handed them to her. He arranged them in her hands, she shifted them around, feeling awkward, and he put them back. She grimaced and held them as Uncle Andrew had showed her, and she tried not to panic when he started to walk away from the horse, unspooling a long lead line.

"Relax," he told her. "Sit straight, but loose."

She couldn't relax, but at least she was already sitting straight. She had won several prizes for posture from Miss Miniver's. She shifted her gaze from the back of Bluebell's head to Uncle Andrew and back again. Her uncle was several paces away now, holding the end of the line, and Bluebell was beginning to anticipate . . . something. Movement, an action of some kind.

"Are you ready?" Uncle Andrew called to her.

"Will I ever be?" Anthea squeaked back.

"Good answer! Hup!"

Uncle Andrew twitched the lead and Bluebell started forward with a jolt.

Anthea dropped one of the reins and grabbed a handful of mane instead. She held on in terror as the horse rocked and

jounced around the paddock. Anthea clamped down with her legs, afraid that she was about to slip sideways out of the highly polished saddle, and Bluebell started to go even faster, every step jarring Anthea until her teeth clacked together.

Now Anthea let go of the other rein and just clung with her legs and hands to the horse. This was not at all like her memories of riding, which had a dreamy quality far different from this horrible reality. Anthea was reminded of the little boat that Uncle Daniel had once rented during their annual seaside holiday. They had only gone a few lengths from shore when Belinda Rose had screamed that she wanted off, and one of the younger girls was sick all over her shoes. Anthea didn't remember which one; she had been too busy fighting to keep her own lunch in her stomach. Riding Bluebell was exactly like that, only Uncle Daniel had turned the boat around and gone back to shore, while Bluebell just went faster and faster . . .

"Whoa, there," Uncle Andrew called.

And faster and faster . . .

"Whoa, girl!"

And faster and faster . . .

"Anthea, tell her to stop!"

And faster and faster and faster until Anthea squeezed her eyes shut and screamed for the beast to stop. Bluebell did, as suddenly as she had started, and the next thing Anthea knew she was on the ground, flat on her back a little in front and to one side of the horse, who was definitely laughing at her.

"Get up, quick now," Uncle Andrew said. He seemed remarkably unconcerned about his niece, who had just done a somersault off a horse, as Anthea opened her mouth to point out. Andrew hauled her to her feet. "Get up, get on her back, *now*," he said in a low voice.

"No! I failed," Anthea said, taking a step back.

The soft earth of the paddock shifted under her feet, and she felt as though she were falling backward for a moment, and had to close her eyes again. She could barely catch her breath.

"Anthea, you must show her that you are in charge. She *will* let you ride her; she will behave as she has been trained."

Anthea gaped at him. How the horse had been trained to behave? What about the way *Anthea* had been trained to behave? Being thrown into the dirt by a monster was not part of Rose Academy training! Anthea was on the verge of arguing with her uncle, but then Bluebell tossed her head and made a sort of chuckling noise.

A tide of rage rose in Anthea. She was not about to be laughed at by some filthy horse with a stupid name. She grabbed the reins and cocked her knee. Andrew scooped it with both hands, and this time she pulled herself up and into the saddle, awkwardly yet without any further humiliation.

"Nice and straight," her uncle said, nodding at her posture. "But hold yourself a little looser. When you squeeze with your legs, you're telling her you want to go faster. Try to move with her; when she bounces up, you bounce up. Use your legs to lift

yourself just a little, up and down, and hold the reins in a firm grip."

Biting back a comment on how she could have used this information the first time around, Anthea merely nodded. Her uncle walked to the center of the paddock once more, pulled the lead line taut, and gave another "Hup!" Anthea squeezed with her knees, but just a little, and Bluebell came to life again.

Anthea tried to read the horse's mood: Was she still laughing? Mostly there was a sense of curiosity. Bluebell was anxious to see what Anthea would do next. Anthea did her best to seem confident, and she concentrated on sending thoughts of going around the paddock in a nice, steady pace. She made sure to concentrate on what the horse was doing and ignore Uncle Andrew.

After five or six times around the paddock, once Anthea had the rhythm of popping up and down with the horse to avoid too many bruises to her buttocks, she was feeling better about her riding, but Bluebell was getting bored again. Anthea dared to squeeze with her knees. Bluebell flicked an ear back, interested, and sped up. Two more rounds at that speed, and Anthea nudged her again, sending thoughts of going fast, but not too fast. Two more rounds.

Now Bluebell was rocking like a ship again, but this time Anthea was surer of herself. Also, falling off hadn't hurt too badly. She loosened the reins a bit to get a more comfortable grip. Bluebell stretched out her neck, and began to go faster.

Suddenly the rocking lessened and they were moving around the paddock at a smooth run, Anthea's brown hair streaming back behind them like Bluebell's white tail.

Somewhere off in another paddock there was a commotion. Bluebell twisted her neck and slowed unevenly. Anthea could tell that the horse was upset by something . . . something about the horse throwing a fit over by the stable, but Anthea wasn't sure what or why.

Anthea managed to keep her seat and send Bluebell comforting thoughts at the same time. She slid her feet out of the stirrups and clamped her legs around the mare, but this time she hauled back on the remaining rein at the same time, shrieking, "Whoa!" and holding to Bluebell's mane with her free hand.

"Excellent!" Uncle Andrew grinned as he came over and helped her recover the rein. "Hold it like this, remember." He redid her grip on the reins. "Now. I'm going to take the lunge line off the bridle, and I want you to follow me back to the stable."

Relieved, Anthea started to twist, wondering how you got off the horse any more gracefully than you got on.

"No, no, I mean, stay there!" Andrew held up a hand. "I want you to guide her back to the stable. Put your feet back in the stirrups, and you can dismount on the block outside the stable. Then I'll show you how to wipe her down and feed her."

Anthea and the horse sighed at the same time, both of them reluctant for the riding lesson to end, which made Uncle

Andrew laugh. Then Anthea had to laugh, too. She was surprised, and pleased, that Bluebell seemed to enjoy being ridden, at least at the end. As she gingerly guided Bluebell toward the stable, she felt a smile splitting her face that wouldn't go away.

It wasn't like flying, not yet, anyway. And she wasn't riding Florian, but still . . . Anthea felt a huge bubble of joy in her chest, just waiting to explode. If she could have carried a tune, she would have burst into song.

Bluebell stopped next to the big tree stump in the stable yard. Anthea looked around, startled. She hadn't noticed that they had reached the "block," as Uncle Andrew called it. The odor of the stable yard filled her nostrils, the smells intensified and made much more welcoming by Bluebell's feelings.

She sighed again, and sat for just a moment before asking how she was supposed to get off. Then, looking across the tops of the fences from her vantage point on Bluebell's back, she saw Florian. He had a man on either side of him, holding a rope attached to his halter.

"What are you doing?" Anthea shouted, even though the men couldn't have heard her.

She somehow got off Bluebell's back without getting entangled in the stirrups or the reins and stormed across the yard toward Florian. He strained his head over the fence, trying to reach her, even as the men tried to pull him away.

"Leave him alone!" Anthea shouted.

"Anthea!" Uncle Andrew said.

She could hear him coming after her. She could see other men stopping to watch as she stomped through the mud, shouting, but she didn't care.

"Stay back, miss," one of the men said as she got closer.

Anthea ignored him and ducked between the slats of the fence. They were dragging Florian back, away from her.

"Let go of him!"

"This horse is dangerous, miss," the man said. "He's been acting up real regular."

"That is *my* horse, and you will let go of him," she ordered.

The men continued to back Florian away. He screamed and pawed at the earth with his front hooves. Had it been any other horse, Anthea would have been terrified, but this was Florian.

"Florian," she said. "Come here!"

Florian reared. The men had to let go of the ropes or be dragged. When he was free he came down and trotted meekly to Anthea. She grabbed hold of his halter and rubbed his forehead, sending waves of calm to him with her touch.

"Hush now," she said. "I'm here."

She glared past him at the men. They were looking at her in astonishment. She turned and saw her uncle standing at the fence behind her. He was shaking his head, but looked resigned.

"From now on, no one touches Florian but Anthea," he told the men.

"But, Captain," one of the men protested. "He went mad! Jumped two fences and tried to stomp on Yates!"

Anthea looked at Florian severely.

"Did you?"

He hung his head. She understood that seeing her riding another horse had been just as hard for him as it had been hard for her to agree to ride Bluebell in the first place.

"I still love you," she said softly to Florian. "But I'm going to ride Bluebell."

"Just . . . leave him to my niece," Uncle Andrew told the men.

Anthea took the lead ropes and led him out to the yard. As she passed Bluebell, she gathered up the mare's reins as well. Bluebell was standing by the block with an expression of what Anthea hoped was respect. Bluebell followed Anthea without Anthea even needing to tug on the reins, moving in to step beside Florian.

Anthea led both horses into the stable. As she passed, one of the riders whistled, his eyes wide. Another took off his cap and bowed. Anthea nodded at the man coolly.

FLORIAN

Florian did his best to calm down, but it was not easy.

Beloved Anthea had come to the paddocks in the early morning, when he had only just eaten his breakfast. She came, but did not look in his direction, though he cried out to her until the men began to fuss around him, telling him to be calm. He could not be calm! Beloved Anthea was within his sight, but would not come to him. She smelled of fear again, as she had when she had first returned.

The Thornley took her to one of the training rings and helped her to mount one of the mares. Florian did not know the mare's name, that was not his place, but he knew her to be of good standing among the other mares. She was a gray, unusual among his kind, and it pleased Florian also to see this distinctive mare carrying Beloved Anthea. He called out to the mare, though it was forward of him, to bring his Beloved toward him. But she, as was her right, ignored him.

But then she allowed Beloved Anthea to fall. Florian screamed with rage, and now two men came and tried to draw him away. The Thornley never once looked his way, nor did Beloved Anthea. Florian could have sworn that the gray mare was laughing at Beloved Anthea's clumsiness.

Florian was so filled with emotion that he hardly knew what he was doing. He reared and kicked, trumpeting his displeasure. The men tried to calm him, to tie a rope to his halter and lead him away. He didn't want to go away; he wanted to go to his Beloved.

The herd stallion's voice cut across the voices of the men. Constantine had seen Florian's shameful rage and demanded that Florian calm himself.

With the greatest of efforts, Florian lowered his head, bowing in shame in the direction of his herd stallion, who glared from his private paddock.

In the stable yard Florian heard the voices of Beloved Anthea and The Thornley, and even with Constantine glaring, Florian dared to call out.

Beloved Anthea came. All was well.

STIFF UPPER...
EVERYTHING

A FEW HOURS LATER, Anthea was doodling on her desk blotter when Jilly knocked on her door.

"Dinner, Anthea!" her cousin called through the door.

"Just a moment; I haven't dressed yet." Anthea put down her pen.

She was supposed to be doing the lessons she had missed from the morning, but she couldn't stop thinking about riding Bluebell. She had been wondering if it would be all that different to ride Florian: he was larger, but she felt closer to him, although the Way enabled her to communicate with both of them.

Anthea had finally set aside the essay she was supposed to be writing about a very maudlin poem, and instead she'd begun writing down everything she had felt and seen and heard and even smelled while she was riding Bluebell. She didn't know why she had written it, or who it was for; she just felt like she needed to tell someone, and Uncle Andrew had been there and seen it all. And she was afraid that Jilly and Finn would just laugh at her for falling off Bluebell.

At first she thought she might send her thoughts to someone back in Coronam in a letter, to tell them about her new life. But to whom could she send it?

She thought of her letter to Aunt Deirdre then, and felt her palms slick with sweat. Anthea wished she had never written, let alone sent, that letter. Perhaps she could send this update to retract what she had said before? Anthea still had not received an answer, though. She was starting to hope that Aunt Deirdre had never received it. Or that she had, but had dismissed the claim of horses being alive as hysteria.

But if Anthea sent a longer letter, one talking about how wonderful the horses were, would that convince Aunt Deirdre to keep their secret? Or maybe it would just be proof that the horses were dangerous, if a young Rose Candidate was now fond of them, riding them, wearing trousers . . .

Anthea sighed. What if she wanted to be a Rose Maiden *and* ride horses? Was that something that could even be?

Jilly knocked on the door again. "Someone hid the dinner gong," she said. "I'm going down now, and so is Papa."

"Oh yes," Anthea said.

Then she stood up.

Or rather, tried to stand up.

"Jillian!" She tried to shout loudly enough for her cousin to hear, but not to sound panicky. It wasn't easy, because she was very panicky. "Um . . . Jilly?"

"What?" Jilly was right outside her door again.

"Help me," Anthea cried.

"What is it?" Jilly rattled the door, which Anthea realized was locked.

"I—I can't move!" Anthea said.

"What? Oh!" And then her cousin started to laugh.

Anthea didn't think it was funny at all. When she had tried to stand up, every muscle in her body had screamed and her spine had locked up. She was half standing now, her rear end just inches from the seat of her desk chair, but she couldn't straighten up or sit down.

There was a scratching sound and Jilly came in. She was still laughing as she tucked a hairpin into her curls.

"Did you pick my lock?" Anthea was watching Jilly from the corner of her eye, since she couldn't turn her head. "Can *everyone* just walk into my room?"

"Well, you wanted me to help you," the other girl said.

She looked at Anthea's awkward pose, and then she gently put a hand on Anthea's elbow and helped her rise. Anthea hissed with pain, and Jilly got her laughing under control.

"Does it feel like this every time you ride?" Anthea wondered how anyone could put up with it.

"No, just the first few times," Jilly assured her. "All the

dance and deportment classes in the world won't prepare your muscles for riding a horse. Or being thrown off one," she added.

Anthea moaned. "You saw?"

"We watched from the classroom."

"*We?*" Anthea froze again, but this time from dread. Then she saw that Jilly wasn't being malicious, she looked . . . proud.

"You got right back on!" Jilly cheered. "Everybody gets thrown the first time. But the real riders get back on."

"That's what Uncle Andrew said," Anthea mumbled.

"And he's always right," Jilly said complacently. "But now we have a problem." She helped Anthea stand in the middle of the room. "We have to get you dressed. Can you lift your arms?"

Anthea tried, but her shoulders felt like they were on fire. She remembered landing on them when Bluebell had thrown her.

"But I felt fine afterward," Anthea whimpered. "And all I've done since then is sit here and read!"

"Your muscles stiffened up while you were sitting," Jilly said.

She went to Anthea's wardrobe and pulled out her gowns. She frowned and discarded them all on the bed.

"The good news is, you can't get into any of these without raising your arms." Jilly had a gleam in her eyes.

"The *good* news?"

"Yes." Jilly closed the wardrobe doors. "The bad news, for you, is that I have just the thing." And she trotted out of the room before Anthea could object.

Anthea tried to breathe deep, but her ribs hurt. She told herself that it couldn't be all that bad.

13

Uncomfortable

IT WAS SO MUCH worse the next morning.

Anthea's muscles had moved past stiffness to pain, and she had to roll out of bed like a log and pull herself upright using the bedpost. She would have stayed in her room and demanded a tray, but Jilly arrived to dress her, and Anthea was too sore to resist. She had been too sore to resist the night before as her cousin crawled all over her, gently taking off Anthea's filthy trousers and shirt—Anthea had not even noticed that she had been wearing the same mannish riding clothes all day.

Jilly had peeled off her dirty clothes without comment, and even washed Anthea's face and hands for her. And then she had presented Anthea with some sort of black slithery thing and the same green Tenduhai robe she herself had been wearing the night before.

"No!" Anthea had said.

"You don't have a choice," Jilly had told her gleefully.

The next thing Anthea knew, her cousin had her dressed in the slippery black thing, which turned out to be a sort of shift that had about a thousand tiny buttons up the back and no sleeves. Then Jilly had slipped the green robe up Anthea's stiff arms and tied the sash tightly around her waist. She put up Anthea's hair with two large ivory combs while Anthea consoled herself that only her uncle and a few others would see her.

She inwardly had to admit that the green color suited her, and that the shift and robe were incredibly comfortable. But she refused to admit, even to herself, that it was rather thrilling to dress in such an exotic manner.

It was just as thrilling the next morning, when Jilly helped her back into the robe, this time over a pair of matching wide-legged Tenduhai trousers. The silk was cool and comfortable, and the cut was flattering. Even if Anthea still felt slightly undressed.

Anthea was so stiff Jilly had to help her up the stairs to the schoolroom. She tried not to let out a scream as she sat down at her desk and instead made a sound like a teakettle about to go on the boil. She fell the last few inches into her seat with a thump.

"Good job yesterday," Keth said, a smile lighting his face.

Anthea let out a little moan. The schoolroom's windows

faced out on the paddocks, and apparently Jilly had not been exaggerating when she said that they had all seen her fall.

"Don't worry about it," Finn said, sitting down beside her. "Everyone falls off the first day. It's one of the laws of the universe." He turned grave, leaning closer. "I didn't think you were going to for a minute, but you always need to get back on."

"Uncle Andrew explained it to me. In a way," Anthea said. She had been so grateful that no one had mentioned her fall at dinner that she had not wanted to ask then.

As Miss Ravel passed back their marked papers, Anthea could sense the anticipation hovering in the air. They were all waiting on her, she realized. They knew that she wanted to ask.

"Why did I have to get right back on?"

"We work *with* the horses," Keth said immediately. "But we also command them. At the same time. It's a delicate balance that must be maintained."

"But once you do find that balance there's nothing else like it in the world," Finn said enthusiastically. "The pairing of horse and person . . . just think of what we could do!"

"I feel like I'm a part of the horse I'm riding," Jilly chimed in, "and I don't even have the Way!"

Her eyes were shining, and for once she didn't look sad or angry about lacking the Way. Anthea smiled back at her. But then the smile faded as Miss Ravel took up the narration.

"That's why the Coronami wanted to get rid of them all," she said.

Anthea's already stiff spine stiffened further as her smile left her face. There it was again, that treasonous talk that made her feel like her clothes didn't fit right.

"Leana wasn't a politically powerful kingdom," Miss Ravel lectured as Anthea clenched her pencil like a weapon. "But with horses and men working together, most of them bonded by the Way, they were a serious threat to the Coronami takeover."

"They didn't take—" Anthea began, but Finn cut her off.

"Actually, they did," he said.

"I know this is hard for you to hear," Miss Ravel continued, "but it is the truth. No one knows where the Coronami came from, but they didn't come from here. This entire land was Leana, from here in the north all the way to the Western Sea, long before it was called Coronam. The Coronami arrived in ships; much the worse for wear after a long journey. They were starving, and many were ill. They were taken in by the Leanans, and then—"

"Then we all died," Finn whispered.

Anthea looked at him.

"The horses got sick first," Finn said to his calloused hands.

"The Leanans got sick, too," Miss Ravel said, taking up the narrative again. "The Coronami, as they recovered, started pushing farther and farther north, until the only remaining people, and horses, were here." She held out her arms to indicate the Last Farm, and the wild lands beyond it.

"When Kalabar built his wall, he told the Leanans it was to keep them safe from whatever illness was in the south, and he told the Coronami that it was to keep them safe from the diseases carried by the horses in the north."

"I don't understand," Anthea said. "Why did they all get sick? The Leanans and the horses, I mean?"

"Dr. Hewett believes the Coronami brought the disease with them. It was probably a common sickness to them, but it devastated this land."

"We aren't a sickly, diseased people!" Anthea protested.

"Exactly!" Jilly said.

"So if the horses got sick, maybe they were going to get sick anyway," she went on, encouraged by her cousin's response.

"Wait, what are *you* talking about?" Jilly frowned.

Finn made a rumbling noise in his throat, but didn't say anything.

"If the Leanans got sick," Anthea explained, trying to work it out as she spoke, "it was probably just a coincidence, because we don't have horrible diseases."

"By 'we' do you mean the Coronami?" Jilly asked.

"Of course," Anthea said.

"Oh, Thea, sweetie," Jilly began.

"Jilly, allow me," Miss Ravel said, with gentle firmness.

"Now, Anthea," Miss Ravel said. "You've taken in so many new ideas since coming here, and I know it's hard. I went through the same thing five years ago. But you're about to learn one more: you're Leanan. If you weren't, you wouldn't have the Way."

Anthea just stared at Miss Ravel. Miss Ravel, with her elegant Travertine accent, and her perfectly smooth chignon.

"I came here to try and talk my brother out of this madness," Miss Ravel said. "He's one of the riders." She didn't conceal the pride in her voice. "He has the Way, and while I do not, I cannot deny that our family has Leanan blood, and that I am just as drawn to the horses as Jeffrey."

"The horses wouldn't let me near them if I wasn't Leanan, at least in part," Jilly chimed in. "Even without the Way, they recognize Leanan blood, and you have to have it, in no small measure, to ride them."

Anthea put her pencil down and rubbed her temples. She had a headache coming on, as though her brain were too full. She looked at Keth, who had been sitting silent this whole time.

"What do you think of all this?"

"What kind of Leanan would I be if I didn't know all this?" He laughed.

Anthea gaped. "But you . . . you're Radiji!" She pointed to his dark-skinned face, as though he were unaware of what he looked like.

"Half Radiji, half Leanan," he said. "You've met my mum, Shannon Taggart."

Anthea blinked. She had indeed met Nurse Shannon, the tall redheaded woman who was Dr. Hewett's "right hand." She simply hadn't realized that she was also Keth's mum. Now that she was looking closer, she saw that he also had freckles, they were just less prominent, and his mother's hazel eyes.

"But . . . but," she stammered. "You honestly believe the Coronami came here, made everyone sick, and then shoved you up here to die?"

Keth nodded. She looked at Finn, who looked back at her, and Anthea knew he believed it as well.

"And we . . . we're all Leanan," she said weakly.

Jilly patted her arm. "Don't worry, I'm sure you're at least a quarter Coronami," she said brightly.

14

TRUCE

ANTHEA PACED HER ROOM. She had just gotten fully unpacked, but she started to pull her dresses out of the wardrobe with restless movements and throw them onto the bed in a wrinkled heap.

Every time someone spoke to her, their words destroyed every truth she had ever known. She felt like her skin didn't fit, and the strange costume she had borrowed from Jilly hardly helped, but she still couldn't move her arms well enough to button herself into anything proper.

The door flew open and Jilly came in. She was like a whirlwind: jewelry jangling, silk rustling, hair in a tangle. She flung herself on Anthea's bed, narrowly missing the gowns.

"Getting ready for a bonfire?" Jilly plucked at the topmost item with her nose wrinkled.

"No," Anthea said. "I'm . . . I don't know what I'm doing! I can't stay here!"

Jilly sat up, realizing that Anthea's distress went beyond stiff muscles. She shoved the gowns aside and folded her legs under her.

"What's wrong?"

Anthea wrestled her trunk out from under the tall bed and put it in the middle of the room. Out of the corner of her eye, she saw the pages she had been writing about her first riding lesson. She tossed a scarf over it.

"Where will you go?" Jilly cocked her head to one side. "You don't have anywhere else."

"Thank you," Anthea said coldly. "Thank for you reminding me of that."

Jilly flushed. "I'm not . . . I didn't want to . . . Are you really running away because we saw you fall off Bluebell?"

Anthea carefully folded her middy blouses. The pain in her back and buttocks made every move agony, but she kept going. She refused to look at Jilly.

"I'm sure everyone back in good ol' Travertine will welcome you with open arms," Jilly went on. "They were so sad when you left! And don't worry: we won't think any less of you because you ran away. Papa won't mind that you turned your back on Leana even though you have the Way, just like your father did. I'm sure your father wouldn't have wanted you to do anything strenuous, and after all, this was only his life's work. You and Florian—"

Jillian was cut off midsentence by one of Anthea's shoes, which struck her on the shoulder with a satisfying *thwack*.

"You did not just do that," Jilly said in a low, dangerous voice.

"Yes, I did!" Anthea's own voice was high and tight. She raised the shoe's mate and took aim.

"How dare you!"

"How dare *I*?"

Anthea threw the other shoe just to get it out of her hand before she started beating her cousin with it. Her throw went wild and the shoe hit the nightstand and knocked a glass onto the floor. It shattered with a sound like a firecracker. Jilly leaped off the bed and came toward Anthea with her fingers curved like claws. Anthea took a step back but didn't stop talking.

"How dare I? Since I came here all you have done is mock me!"

"I tried to be your friend and you rejected me," Jilly countered, still poised as if to strike. "I let you wear my favorite clothes, and I didn't tell anyone that it was because your rump was sore!"

With a whiplash of guilt, Anthea remembered Jilly trying to hug her that first morning, her concern when Anthea had been in Florian's stall, and the gentle way that her cousin had helped dress her since her riding lesson.

Anthea shook off the guilt quickly, however.

"Can't you understand that this is all too strange to me?"

she half shouted, half pleaded. "All my life I've been taught that Coronam has existed since . . . the dawn of time! And that horses died because they were filled with disease, but I come here and you all tell me that's wrong. There are kings, kings who look like regular boys! Kings I've never heard of, and I memorized the names of all the kings of Coronam to the tenth generation!

"I'm wrong, everything I know is wrong, and the life I wanted—to be a Rose Maiden like my dead mother, who isn't dead—is stupid and wrong!"

"Can you understand how *I* feel," Jilly countered. "When you come here from the big city to tell me everything *I've* been taught is wrong and the life *I* want is stupid and wrong?"

Anthea was still shaking, only now her anger had subsided. She saw enormous tears hovering on her cousin's long lashes.

"But do you see . . . I don't know what to do?" Anthea whispered. "I mean, my mother isn't dead, but where is she? How do I find her? Whom do I ask for help?"

"No one knows where your mother is," Jilly said. "She . . . she does something for the Crown, something secret. But at least she has a reason for staying away, unlike mine."

"What?" No one had ever mentioned an Aunt Anything, so Anthea had assumed that Jilly's mother was long dead. "Your mother? She . . . ?"

"Lives in Travertine," Jilly said with a shrug that made a tear fall onto her lap. "She doesn't like horses, you see. Or having a daughter who likes horses."

"Oh, Jillian . . . Jilly!"

Anthea reached out for her cousin, but the other girl brushed her aside angrily.

"I'd give anything to be you," Jilly said. "No mother sending you preachy letters saying that you can come 'home' if you agree to act like a lady. No one but yourself to please. And the *Way* . . ." Her voice cracked with longing.

Anthea crossed to the window and whipped aside the curtain. "And I'd like to be *you*," she said with a heat that surprised her. "No rules, you can do as you like. You can dress like a boy, eat chocolates all day, stay up all night reading novels. Spend your days with horses without fear." She sucked in a heaving breath. "You don't have to read your mother's letters, but at least she sends you letters!"

"Why does that make you so angry?"

"Because I'm jealous," Anthea blurted out, surprising both of them this time. There was a heartbeat's pause, and then Anthea added, "And scared."

"Of the horses?"

"Of making my own decisions," Anthea told her. "What if I'm wrong? What if I decide it's all right to use the Way, but then I find out . . ."

"Find out what?" Jilly's voice shook. "That you don't have the Way after all? You know that's not true. But now you have to learn to use it."

"But what if . . . what if I . . . ruin everything?" Anthea's heart pounded. The corner of stationery still visible on her desk seemed to taunt her.

"Don't be vain," her cousin scoffed. "I doubt you could ruin *everything.*"

"But it's so hard!" Anthea's voice ended in a wail.

Jilly sighed. "I do understand. I've always wanted to have the Way, you've always wanted to be a Rose Maiden. If I had the Way and it was taken from me, I'd be inconsolable."

The cousins stood, contemplating each other, for a long time.

"It would be nice to have my cousin back," Jilly said finally. "The one who used to like me."

"I do like you," Anthea said.

"Truce?" Jilly held out her hand to shake, but Anthea startled them both by hugging her, though the action made her whimper.

"Help me clean up?" Anthea begged. "I can't move!"

"Only if I can turn that brown dress into dusting cloths. I mean, what were you thinking? And the pink sashes! You're not five years old!"

Anthea surprised them both again by laughing.

FLORIAN

Beloved Anthea was still not permitted to ride him, but Florian contented himself with her constant attention. Beloved Anthea was with him every day, caring for him, feeding him, and letting him run in the paddock alongside her as she learned to ride the gray mare. For now that was good enough, because his Beloved was so happy. The mare had even condescended to tell Florian that her name was Bluebell, and she had confessed a growing fondness for Beloved Anthea, which pleased Florian greatly.

Florian knew that one day his Beloved Anthea would ride him. Perhaps when the Soon King took the reins of the herd stallion. But as long as no one tried to take his Beloved away from him again, he was content.

15

HIDING WITH FLORIAN...AGAIN

NOW THAT SHE NO longer hid from her riding lessons, Anthea spent much more time with Jilly as well as with Finn and Keth, and she found that she liked them.

Anthea had never met a group of young people so free and easy in their ways. They never worried about their reputations, had no sense of decorum, and didn't care that Anthea seemed to find every mud puddle with her boots or that her hair tended to slip and coil out of its ribbon and stick to her face. They attended their morning lessons and studied together over lunch, laughing and chatting. Every afternoon they went out to the paddocks to ride, and sometimes they fell off.

Except for Finn. Finn never fell off his horse, a sort of steel-gray speckled beast—what the others called a blue roan—named Marius.

Anthea had never spent so much time in the company of

boys her own age before. She was often startled when they spoke to her, calling her by her first name, or bumped into her in the aisles of the stable or in the classroom. Finn especially made her feel sort of fluttery, a sensation that was both pleasant and unnerving.

It didn't help that they took special lessons from Caillin MacRennie, just the two of them.

Sometimes they rode to the far edges of the farm, where the horses in the paddocks looked no bigger than dots, and Caillin asked them how many horses were in each paddock, which were mares and which stallions. He would have them turn their backs, spin three times, and point directly to Constantine when they stopped. Anthea felt deeply foolish doing most of these things. Especially because Finn was never wrong. She also couldn't see the point in his watching her dry heave the first time she tried to feel what Florian was doing and gagged on the taste of the grass he was eating.

But the most thrilling and yet terrifying exercise was the one that involved Caillin MacRennie taking the bridle off Bluebell and telling Anthea to guide her using only the Way. He would tell her, where Bluebell couldn't hear, that he wanted her to make the mare walk forward, turn left, turn right, trot, and then stop, or some such combination. The memory of her first riding lesson, of feeling herself completely lose control of Bluebell, made Anthea feel green with fear. More than once Bluebell just sat there as though she had no idea that Anthea was even trying to talk to her. More than twice Finn and Marius had to catch them up, and Finn had to take control of Bluebell to make her stop.

"Can't I do this with Keth instead?" Anthea whispered to Caillin MacRennie one day.

"Keth's done as much as he can with the Way," Caillin MacRennie said. "Like most of us, he can feel horses nearby, and he can make them do what he asks, if he asks nicely. But you and Finn, now . . . that's something else."

"Is it?" Anthea's voice raised in surprise.

She had thought that you either had the Way or didn't. She had assumed that Keth and Caillin MacRennie and Miss Ravel's brother Jeffrey all felt Constantine's pride and rage, that their stomachs all growled when the foals went to their breakfasts. But that was not the case.

"There's not been anyone as sensitive as you two in a long time," Caillin MacRennie told her.

"None of my family have dared to ride a herd stallion, to really take control of the herd, in generations," Finn said softly. "But I . . . I can feel Constantine's moods all the time."

Anthea finally asked something that had been bothering her.

"I thought my father rode Constantine? Jilly once said that she and I rode him, too, as children."

"Aye, before Justinian died our Con wasnae quite the arrogant b-beast," Caillin MacRennie said, catching himself with a grin and a wink. "Just another stallion in the herd, back then."

"And Justinian was Florian's father?" Anthea asked.

Finn and Caillin MacRennie both nodded.

"Con and Florian are half brothers," Finn added.

"And Justinian was the old herd stallion? I thought he was my father's horse?"

Herd politics made her brain hurt, but she was determined to learn. Her father hadn't been a king, or claimed to be a king . . . had he? Yet everyone said that only Finn would be able to ride Constantine, though he hadn't yet dared to try. Anthea didn't understand what people thought would happen when Finn finally did ride Constantine, but that was the one thing she knew she would never dare to ask.

"Justinian was of a more easygoing nature than Con," Caillin MacRennie said.

"And he paid for it," Finn said under his breath.

"What? What do you mean?"

Anthea had been riding Bluebell in a tight circle around Marius in one of the far paddocks. She was trying to control the mare with just her knees, giving her brain and the Way a rest, but now she grabbed the reins and pulled up to look at Finn.

He looked at Caillin MacRennie, who gave him an encouraging nod.

"You become the herd stallion by defeating the herd stallion," he told her.

"In a race, you mean?"

All the riders loved to race. Sometimes they also leaped their horses over low walls or bales of hay, and the winner didn't have to muck stalls for a week.

"No," Finn said with obvious reluctance. "In a fight. Con challenged Justinian when he was full grown and Justinian was starting to get old. They fought and Con won."

"They . . . fought?"

Bluebell stamped and kicked out with one of her hind legs, feeling Anthea's disquiet.

"How badly was Justinian hurt?"

She knew what Finn was going to say, but she wanted to hear him say it.

"He died."

Bluebell lurched forward. Anthea grabbed the reins but let her go. She could sense Marius and Finn just behind her, and Caillin MacRennie on Gaius Julius, but they didn't try to stop her.

She raced Bluebell across the far pasture, telling the mare to pull up only when they reached the fence where Florian waited patiently. Anthea called him over with a thought and petted his head ferociously, like she would a dog, while she caught her breath.

"That seems like enough for now," Caillin MacRennie said. "Back to the stables with you all."

Finn pushed open the gate for Anthea and Bluebell, and

they collected Florian and headed back to meet up with Jilly and Keth, who were having a wet-sponge fight that felt entirely too frivolous. Anthea could not understand how they could know what they did about Constantine, and stallions fighting to the death, and then fling water at each other like children at the seaside.

Finn saw her scowl and caught a sponge in midair before it could hit her. She didn't even thank him; she just led Florian to his stall in silence.

But when she came back out, he was waiting. He tossed the large, sopping sponge he had just taken from Keth right over her shoulder. It smacked into the wall between Florian's and Marius's stalls and slid squishily to the floor.

"It's going to be okay," he told her. "Relax."

Anthea picked up the sponge and glared at him. Finn ducked into one of the stalls. After a minute, he leaned back out with a smirk on his tanned face.

"They don't teach Rose Maidens to throw, I'll bet," he teased.

"Physical education is very important for young ladies," Anthea said, her voice prim. Then she pulled back to her ear the way she had been taught, threw, and hit Finn directly in the face.

There was an intake of breath from Jilly, and even Finn was shocked into silence. Keth, who had been hiding in another stall, came out into the open, his jaw slack.

Jilly slowly collapsed onto a stool with a noise like a bag-piper warming up. Anthea clutched her throat, terrified at the thought that she had even shocked her cousin. Finn was a king! What had she been thinking?

Finn took a step toward her, and Anthea quailed. He stooped and picked up the still sopping sponge, not even bothering to wipe the water and suds off his face. He raised his arm, threw, and the sponge smacked into the back of Jilly's head.

"Hey!" She leaped to her feet. "What was that for?"

"For laughing at me!"

"I knew it!" Jilly shrieked. "You won't hit Anthea because you think she's beautiful!"

Anthea remembered the argument Finn and Jilly had been having the day that she had found Florian, and her face turned red. To cover her embarrassment, she took up another sponge, but she found that she couldn't hit Finn again, and she didn't want to anger Jilly (not that she thought her cousin was really angry), so instead she threw it at Keth. But rather weakly, and it smacked again the shin of his riding boot.

"Hey! What did I do?" he demanded, but he took aim at Anthea, and she fled.

She ducked into Florian's stall and rubbed his neck with one hand. With her other she fished in her pocket for a hoof pick and the others continued the barrage of soapy sponges.

"Ah, not you lot again!" One of the men had come into the

stable, and he shouted down the row of stalls in agitation. "Stop makin' such a mess!"

"Sorry, sir," Keth squeaked.

"It's just soap," Jilly said, sounding completely innocent. "We're cleaning the whole stable, all at once."

"So thoughtful," the man said, sounding exasperated. "But you had better get this cleaned up before that little Rose Maiden happens by."

"Why?" Jilly said.

Anthea straightened. Her sudden unease made Florian whicker and stamp. She didn't dare shush him aloud, so she sent him soothing thoughts instead. To reinforce it, she braced her boots against the stable wall and put her upper body over his back, so that her weight was hanging off him. It was the best way she could think to give a horse his size a physical as well as mental hug.

She wanted to hear what the rider had to say. From the silence of the others she guessed they wanted to hear it, too, because no one told him she was there.

"The last thing we need is her reporting back that we're not only breeding horses, but we're letting a bunch of young hooligans ride them!"

"Reporting?" Finn asked. "To whom would she report?"

"Does it matter? She's already written at least one letter back to her aunt and uncle. Her aunt was a Rose Maiden; her uncle works in the Home Office. Either way it's bad news for the Last Farm."

"She wouldn't, would she? She wouldn't tell them about the horses!" Keth didn't sound very certain, though.

"Of course she wouldn't," Jilly said staunchly. "She probably just wanted her aunt and uncle to know she got here safely."

Anthea pushed off from the wall a little more so that she was lying across Florian's back more comfortably. She tangled her fingers in his mane.

"I did write a letter," she whispered to Florian. "But I wish I hadn't."

He flicked an ear at her, but his loving thoughts didn't waver. He wasn't anxious about the letter, so she tried to copy him.

"I still wouldn't put a toe out of line around that one," the man said. "The daughter of Genevia Cross is no innocent miss."

"Anthea's mother is Genevia *Cross*?" Keth's voice cracked.

"Thornley," Anthea added in a whisper. Florian flicked an ear back.

"Anthea thought she was dead," Jilly said. "And how do *you* know her mother's name?" she asked Keth, who mumbled an answer that Anthea couldn't hear.

"Ha! Like anyone could kill Genevia Cross!" The man snorted.

"Thornley," Anthea said again, a little louder this time.

She threw a leg over Florian and sat up on his back. She just needed to sit on him for a minute.

"She was born here. Her father used to run Last Farm," Jilly said. "And she's here because *my* father sent for her."

Silence.

"Now, why don't you let us clean up the mess we've made?" Jilly's voice sounded sweet, but Anthea could hear the steel within it.

The rider must have left, because everyone fell silent. Anthea sat on Florian, thinking. At last Jilly appeared, looking over the half door of the stall at Anthea. She turned away and came back with a bridle.

"Keep him to a walk," she said, holding it out.

"Jilly!" Keth yelled. "Are you letting her ride Florian?"

"I won't tell if you won't," Jilly said coolly.

Florian stepped closer, and Jilly slipped the bridle over his head.

"Jilly!"

"Be quiet, Keth," Finn said. "Keep to the east paddock," he added, passing by Florian's stall and stopping to pick up a thrown sponge.

"Why is Keth afraid of my mother?" she asked, her voice barely a whisper.

Jilly looked just as baffled. But as Finn walked past again with his collection of sponges, he looked at her carefully for a minute and then said, "The rumor is that she is no longer considered a Rose Matron. Not because she did anything . . . scandalous, but because she defied the queen in order to work for the king."

"I don't understand," Anthea said, feeling a dull headache start behind her furrowed eyebrows. "Work for the king as what?"

"As a spy," Finn said simply. "She's his personal spy."

16

THE OWL IN THE PADDOCK

SOMEONE KNOCKED AT ANTHEA'S bedroom door that evening. They told her they were leaving a tray in the hall, if she felt like eating, poor mite.

Anthea got up and opened her window. It was dark outside, but the gray stones of the house jutted out from the mortar and were covered in a climbing vine as well, an old one that was nearly as thick as Anthea's arm in places. Climbing nets were also commonly used in physical education classes at Miss Miniver's. Anthea swung her leg out and clambered down.

The horses were stabled for the night; she could feel their thoughts of hay and oats and sleep. Several of them, woken by Anthea and her distress, stuck their heads over their stall doors as she passed. She only paused to pat Bluebell as she went down the aisle, straight to Florian's stall.

As soon as he had nuzzled her head in welcome, and made sure that she wasn't hurt, he lay down in the thick straw of his stall. She sighed. It was just what she had needed. Uncle Andrew had come into the stables and stopped her from riding Florian earlier, and instead she had just walked him around the paddock like a dog. It wasn't the same as riding him, even though they had been able to share thoughts of love and he had soothed some of her turmoil.

She sat in the straw and leaned her back against his warm, broad side. He sent her soothing thoughts, and images of walking together under sunny skies, and she tried to return the favor despite her swirling thoughts.

The sound of riders moving about the stable woke her the next morning. Anthea was embarrassed to find herself still in the frock she had put on for dinner the night before, only to decide she couldn't face the others in the dining room. It was hopelessly crumpled and she had straw in her hair and drool on her cheek. She hurried to wipe her face on her sleeve and get Florian to his feet.

She put on his halter and led him out of the stall, trying to look as though she had just arrived early to put him in the paddock, lace-trimmed frock and all. She nodded cordially to the riders she passed, keeping her eyes on the ground, and pretended that she wasn't the cause of their startled faces. Normally she walked with her shoulders back, eyes forward, like a lady, but today she just didn't have the strength, so she studied the patterns of the hoof and boot prints in the mud of the stable yard.

There was another set of prints that she couldn't identify. Small, almost like a chicken's, but not. Anthea's arm was jerked roughly as Florian stopped dead before she could bump into the fence around Constantine's paddock.

She looked up and blinked. She had been so intent on trying to figure out what sort of creature had made the marks that she had a crick in her neck. Constantine was on the far side of his enclosure watching the mares moving out of the stable in a neat row, led by Jilly, who gave Anthea a wave.

Anthea waved back and then returned her gaze to the ground. Florian pulled at her arm, worried about her odd behavior, but she refused to move. She had just seen what had made the tracks, and she felt a little bubble of laughter rising in her chest.

It was a tiny burrowing owl. Anthea had seen their holes on some of her rides, but she had never seen one of the owls outside of a book. She had just taken Jilly's word for it that they existed. While southern owls were large majestic tree dwellers, these northern birds were little round things with eyes nearly too big for their bodies. They could fly but preferred to live underground.

Now to her delight there was one marching across the ground right in front of her. And there was no other word for it: the little brown-and-gray bird was marching, wings tucked back, as though it had important business waiting for it. Anthea laughed out loud, and the owl shook its head in annoyance.

Constantine had been facing the opposite direction, but at the sound of Anthea's laugh he wheeled around. His black obsidian eyes fixed on the owl. Anthea saw his entire body tense with rage at the intrusion in *his* paddock.

"No!" Anthea shouted. "Don't you dare!"

Constantine tossed his head, not even deigning to look at Anthea. Anthea dropped Florian's lead, and Florian made a noise that was the horse equivalent of her own shout of denial. He snapped his teeth, trying to grab her by the sleeve, but it was too late. Anthea slipped through the bars of the fence and ducked into Constantine's paddock, leaving Florian's teeth to click together on the air where she had just been.

She straightened and faced Constantine. He glanced at her, but both of their gazes went immediately to the owl. For its part, the little bird was still stumping along, either unaware of or simply ignoring them.

"Leave it," Anthea said, the way she would to a dog that was after a cat.

A surge of anger came from Constantine, and Anthea knew that she had done exactly the wrong thing. Florian's fear struck her a second later, and she took an involuntary step back.

Constantine struck like a snake. Lashing out with a single hoof, he sent the owl flying. The little bird made a sharp cry, and so did Anthea. Constantine reared onto his hind legs and took a hop forward, putting himself in position to bring both front hooves down on the ragged ball of feathers.

"No!"

Anthea screamed and leaped forward. She scooped up the owl and tucked it into the crook of one arm. She raised the other arm, hand flat to Constantine and gave another shout.

"Stop! Halt! Whoa!"

She reached out with her mind, as she would have to Florian. Constantine had no thoughts of love, no thoughts of kindness or the joy of running or the pleasure of a warm stall. His thoughts were like a black hedge of thorns. But still, Anthea pushed against them, willing him to leave her, and the owl, in peace.

"Leave us alone, you . . . you . . . great *bully*!"

Constantine froze mid-rear. The whole stable yard froze, the sounds of men and horses stopping abruptly. Anthea heard someone curse, a dreadful word, and was certain it was Jilly's voice, but Anthea didn't flinch or take her eyes off the hooves over her head. She didn't take her mind off pushing the stallion away.

And then Florian was there. He leaped the fence and charged, calling a challenge at Constantine. Anthea screamed herself, terror for Florian chilling her heart and breaking her concentration.

A wave of shock passed over her and Constantine stumbled

back and away from Florian. His front hooves came down an arm's length from Anthea and she nearly fainted from the emotions battering at her from both horses.

From Constantine: anger.

From Florian: terror.

Constantine screamed and lashed at Florian with his forelegs. Anthea curled into a ball around the owl and waited to feel one of those steel-shod hooves come down on her head. She knew she was going to die; she prayed that Florian, at least, would live.

And the owl. It would be much better if she died saving the owl, instead of just dying with it.

"You idiot!"

Hands grabbed her shoulders. Someone was dragging her along the ground. She kept her arms around the owl and scuffed out with her boots, helping whoever it was to move her to the paddock fence. She dared to raise her head and look at the horses, and she saw Constantine bite Florian's neck with his yellow teeth.

She tried to shake off the hands. Whoever it was clamped down tighter and half dragged, half threw her against the fence. He let go and came around between her and the stallions, and Anthea saw that it was Finn. His face was chalky white as he pushed her head between her shoulders, and then shoved her ignominiously under the lowest rail.

Constantine came thundering toward them, seeing that

Anthea was about to escape, and Finn rolled under the fence just in time. Constantine lashed at the boards, trying to break through to get at them. Finn stumbled to his feet, hauled Anthea up, and pushed her toward an anxious knot of people standing to one side.

"But what about Florian?" Anthea panted. She tried to stop, to turn.

"Florian knows what he has to do," Finn said grimly. "And so do I," he added, under his breath.

Anthea hurried to the opposite fence and climbed through, ripping her skirt in the process. Jilly helped her, but when Anthea turned back to lend her free hand to Finn, she saw that he had gone back into Constantine's paddock.

"What is he doing?" She lurched back to the fence, but now it was Jilly holding her back. Anthea accidentally clutched the owl too tight in her left hand, and it screeched and bit her thumb. She ignored the pain as she turned to watch Finn and Florian. Her stomach dropped into her shoes and she thought her heart was going to burst.

"Florian!" she shouted. "No!"

Jilly wrapped an arm around her shoulders. "It'll be all right," she said in an unconvincing voice.

"He has to do this," Uncle Andrew said, sounding like he was telling himself more than Anthea.

They all watched as Finn slowly walked toward the fighting stallions. Anthea could no longer differentiate between the stallions' emotions; their turmoil was a thick cloud, almost visible. Finn was tall, and strong from working with horses all his life, but he looked tiny as he walked toward Constantine.

Florian turned and looked at Anthea. Then he dropped his head and stood in front of Constantine, waiting.

"No," Anthea whispered.

Constantine reared onto his hind legs again. He screamed his war cry.

Florian did not move.

"No," Finn said, his voice clear and firm. "Come down."

Constantine came down, not on top of Florian, but certainly very close. He paced around the other stallion, strutting, his tail flagged out and his ears pricked.

Florian did not move. Neither did Finn.

Constantine struck with a front hoof, gouging at the back of one of Florian's hind legs. He bared his teeth and bit Florian on the shoulder.

"No," Finn said again. "You're done."

Constantine backed up a single step.

Tears poured down Anthea's face. Uncle Andrew hurried to the paddock gate and swung it open. Florian heaved a shuddering sigh and limped out while Constantine looked on. Finn lifted one hand, but stopped short of touching the herd stallion. Then he turned and followed Florian out of the paddock.

"I hate Constantine," Anthea blurted out.

"He has to keep control of the herd," Finn said, closing the gate.

He looked exhausted, and Anthea wondered what he had been doing with the Way to keep Constantine from killing him and Florian both.

"Florian defied him," Finn said. "But Florian isn't strong enough to win a fight with Con, so he had to be the one to back down. He had to take his punishment."

"Why?" Anthea sobbed.

"The herd stallion is their king," Jilly said. "The other horses listen to people because he tells them they have to. It would be chaos without him."

Anthea ran to her poor horse. Blood was streaming from half a dozen wounds.

She reached out and found she was still holding the owl, which was still biting her. She unclamped its beak from her thumb and stuffed it into her jacket. Then she put both her hands, one of them streaming blood, on Florian's forehead.

"My darling," she whispered. "I'm so sorry."

He sighed mightily and raised his head just enough to lean it on her shoulder.

Constantine had thought for even a second that Florian wanted to challenge him. No, Constantine had known that Florian only wanted to protect his Beloved Anthea, and so had spared his life.

But it hurt. His leg. His neck. His shoulder.

And his pride.

Florian had never been chastised by the herd stallion before. He would, of course, defend Beloved Anthea again, even if it meant his death.

Nevertheless, his pride was stung.

He limped to the barn with Beloved Anthea at his side, fussing over him. It made him feel marginally better. Until she pulled an injured ground owl out of her clothing and perched it on his water bucket.

FLORIAN

Beloved Anthea had nearly been killed.

She had trespassed in the herd stallion's private paddock. But still . . .

Florian could not have lived if she had been killed.

And so he had defied his herd stallion.

It would have been within Constantine's right to destroy Florian. It would have prevented him from losing his status among the other stallions. But the Soon King had gotten Beloved Anthea out of the way, and so Florian was able to show his submissiveness to the herd stallion. He had no desire to fight Constantine. He had no desire to replace him. All he wanted was for his Beloved Anthea to be safe.

Constantine had not said a word to Florian, but Florian knew the herd stallion understood. Florian would be dead now if

ANOTHER LETTER

FLORIAN DIDN'T LIKE THE little owl, but Anthea didn't care. Its wing had been injured, and she felt responsible for it, so she was determined to nurse it back to health despite Florian's sighs and dirty looks. She had explained to Florian, using words and images, that the reason why she had gone into Constantine's paddock was to save the bird, and leaving it to die would render his own injuries futile, and she knew that he understood. But he still sighed whenever he saw the bird.

❧

"Why *Arthur*, though?" Jilly asked.

"Look at his face," Anthea said. "He's clearly an Arthur!"

The little owl nipped lovingly (and much more gently) at Anthea's fingers. She had a bandage around her left hand, covering the gouge where Arthur had bitten her during the incident the day before. She was worried that she would have a scar, but Dr. Hewett had given her an ointment that he said should make it minimal.

Then he had shown Anthea how to wrap the owl's wing tightly to his body, though that was easier said than done. The little owl was almost but not quite spherical; his feathers were very slick. But Dr. Hewett, who was rarely excited about anything, was very excited by Arthur.

"I kept one as a boy," he had told Anthea. "They make capital pets!"

Florian didn't think so, but Anthea was still determined to nurse Arthur back to health. And the owl seemed to have no objection. He enjoyed being carried in the crook of her arm, surveying the world from such grand heights. He sat politely on her desk during morning lessons, and rode on Bluebell's pommel during the afternoon. Bluebell didn't mind him at all, or perhaps she was just ignoring him. Either way, they seemed fine together.

Anthea was feeling positively chipper as she went back to her room to dress for dinner. Until she saw the letter waiting for her there.

It was sitting in the middle of her desk, looking completely innocent and completely wrong at the same time. The thick red wax seal stared at Anthea from the backdrop of creamy linen paper like a baleful eye.

She needed to hurry and dress for dinner. She had taken extra care with Florian, having to groom around his bruises and bites from the fight the day before. But the sight of the letter stopped her dead. A glance at the unfamiliar seal was no more reassuring. A rose, with something above it. It could be from any Rose Maiden except Aunt Deirdre, who used a rose surrounded by a *C* for "Cross."

When she picked up the envelope and studied the seal, Anthea felt her mouth go dry. The seal was a rose, and a crown. Anthea dropped into the chair, the letter shaking in her hand.

It took her three attempts with her letter opener to break the seal. She nearly stabbed herself in the wrist in the process, but she finally got it open. The stationery within bore a gold monogram so complex she couldn't decipher it, and more crowned roses ran along the bottom of the first two pages. After that there were another two pages, on thinner paper and with no seal or monogram.

She read the rose-and-crown pages first.

My dear Miss Cross-Thornley,

We have never met but your aunt Deirdre Cross has shared your letter with me, and I have been gathering more information about you from her. I had no idea that Genevia Cross-Thornley, who was once my most trusted Rose Maiden, had a daughter. I wish that I had, because spending your childhood being handed from one distant relative to another cannot have been easy.

Of course, the fact that she had a child was just one of many things that Genevia did not tell me. For instance, she also did not mention that her husband had been guarding the last of the Leanan horses.

Anthea had to stop and get her breath. The *queen*. *The* queen. This letter was from the *queen* of *Coronam*. The queen now knew Anthea existed. The queen now knew that horses existed. But there was nothing in the words that told Anthea how Her Majesty felt about either of those things.

She read on, although her hands were shaking so badly it was hard to keep the paper steady enough to read:

This is all very problematic, for reasons that I don't think it wise to share. At least not just yet. But I will tell you this, and I need you to tell your uncle Andrew Thornley as well. Before Deirdre showed me your letter, she showed it to her husband. And Daniel, I am certain, showed it to my husband.

Please do not write any more letters about Leana and her horses to anyone. Not to your aunt and uncle, not to your cousins or school friends. Not even to me. It is safer for them that way.

I look forward to meeting you someday.

With all best wishes,
Josephine, Queen of Coronam

PS: I have enclosed a letter of your mother's that came into my possession some years ago. I thought you might find it illuminating.

Anthea had to put her head down on the edge of the desk for a moment. The queen knew about the horses. The king knew about the horses. How bad was this? How much danger had Anthea put her uncle and Florian in by writing that letter?

She set the letter carefully aside. She needed to show it to Uncle Andrew immediately, but she also needed to see her mother's letter. She needed to see that first and figure out what the queen had meant by her finding it illuminating.

Anthea had never seen a letter from her mother before. Her mother, the not actually dead, apparently no longer a Rose Maiden, possible spy.

My dear Custard,

Anthea read the greeting a few times, confused. Custard? Was that a nickname for Anthea's father, Charles? It seemed so.

Although it greatly pains me to say it, I fear I shall not be coming home this winter. The reason for my delay cannot, naturally, be written. I know that you shall simply assume that it is everything to do with you and your little project, *but I assure you that it is not. After all, you are not the only one in the family with their life's work to protect these days.*

Speaking of your life's work: was your plan successful? Are the "foals" quite as close as you had hoped? I must say, again, that I still hold many reservations about your plan, but I suppose I can have no vote to the contrary. I did, after all, leave her in your care.

The dinner gong sounded, and Anthea leaped straight up out of her seat. She automatically began to take off the middy blouse she was wearing with her riding trousers, but then she sank back down in her chair and continued to read.

I fail to see how this brainchild of yours will do anything to sway the minds of the Powers That Be. In point of fact, it may very well have the opposite effect.

Perhaps if you can tear yourself away, we might take a brief holiday in the spring. We could meet at the seaside at some halfway point.

Your loving Gen

Anthea checked the date on the letter. In two months' time her parents . . . well, her father at least . . . would be dead. It suddenly struck her like a cold knife in the heart that the train had gone off the rails near Seatowne, in the spring. Had he been on his way to a romantic seaside holiday with her mother when he had died?

Where had her mother been? On another train, traveling north to meet him, Anthea supposed. She had assumed all her life that both her parents had died on the same train, that, like any good wife, her mother had been at her father's side.

And where had Anthea been? She realized that she must have been here, at the farm. Anthea was no doubt the "she" who had been left in her father's care. She had probably been playing with Florian when her father had died. She had no memory of that time, and she wondered if it had been Uncle Andrew who had told her the news.

"Thea?" Uncle Andrew's voice came through the door.

Anthea dropped the letter. She felt like she had been caught doing something wrong. Before she called for him to come in, she shoved both letters under her desk blotter.

"C-c-come in," she finally said.

Her uncle was dressed for dinner, looking quite handsome. Jilly looked a good deal like him, in a feminine way, of course. Anthea thought Jilly's mother probably found that irritating.

"May I sit down?" her uncle asked.

Anthea waved him to the big chair by the fire. She sat back down at her desk, turning the chair with a great deal of ridiculous hopping, until she was facing him.

"Now that we've all had time to think," Uncle Andrew said.

"We were not expecting you to come to us with not only the revulsion you have for horses, but also with no knowledge of your past here or of your parents.

"And you, of course," he went on, raising a hand so that Anthea wouldn't interrupt, even though she had no idea what to say. "You have had a number of shocks since coming here. Everything from learning that your mother is alive to finding yourself seated across from a king at dinner."

"Finding out that you all think my mother is a spy," Anthea added.

"Precisely," Uncle Andrew said. "And as much as I would like to lie to you and let you come to terms with your mother being alive before you had to worry about her being a spy, I'm afraid that I can't. Not anymore."

"What do you mean?"

Her uncle closed his eyes. He looked no less handsome, but a great deal more tired. He patted the breast of his jacket, and Anthea heard a crackle: there was a letter in the inside pocket. But he didn't take it out.

"Hurry and change for dinner," he said, eyes still closed. "We have a lot more to discuss.

"The Crown has discovered Last Farm."

COUNCIL OF WAR

ANTHEA WOULD HAVE THOUGHT that only the adults would gather to discuss what this all meant, but it seemed that, like dinner, war councils were matters for the entire family. And they involved food, because Caillin MacRennie refused to hear bad news on an empty stomach.

So, in addition to Uncle Andrew, Caillin MacRennie, Jilly, Anthea, and Finn, they were joined at the big dining table by Miss Ravel, Dr. Hewett, Nurse Shannon, who brought Keth, and an angry man named Perkins, who seemed to hate everyone and everything, except horses.

As the maids brought in the food, Uncle Andrew took a letter out of his jacket and spread it on the table. He cleared his throat twice before speaking, while they all looked on expectantly.

"This letter is from—"

"The queen?" Anthea blurted out, before she could stop herself.

Uncle Andrew gave her a startled look. "No, why would the queen . . . ? No, it's from a school friend of mine, Mark Castellani," he told them. "He works in the Home Office now. I always suspected that he knew what Charles and I were doing, but he's never said a word about it. Now he's written to say that the king has heard about our farm, and 'what we have on it.' He is quick to assure me that he has never said a word to the king, or anyone higher up, about us. He has no idea who did leak the information, and I believe him.

"And the king is, apparently, not happy."

"So? I fail to see how that fat blowhard's happiness affects us," Perkins said. He turned his attention to his food.

Anthea gasped. Perkins looked at her and rolled his eyes. Finn put a hand on her arm and gave it a reassuring squeeze.

"I know, I know, it's hard," he whispered. "But . . . you'll be fine," he finished lamely.

Anthea did not know if she would be fine, but she didn't shake off Finn's hand. After a moment, he removed it so that he could keep eating. She could still feel where he had touched her. And she had completely lost her appetite. But that had more to do with the letter that she had received, which she felt was glowing like a beacon up in her bedroom.

She had not yet shown it to Uncle Andrew. The letter said to show it to *him*, not to the entire family and all their associates. She didn't want Jilly, or Finn, or Caillin MacRennie to know what she'd done. She didn't want to see the hurt or betrayal in their eyes. She didn't want to hear what Jilly would say when she found out it was Anthea who had told their secret. As soon as her uncle had said he was having a "council of war" over dinner, he had gone out to let her dress, and so she hadn't had a moment alone with him to show him the queen's letter.

Or so she justified it.

"Sir, what do you think the king will do?" Finn asked.

"That is an excellent question, and the one we most need to worry about," Uncle Andrew said. "King Gareth is not a man who likes secrets, unless they are his. Finding out that there is a secret farm, full of horses, after believing them dead for centuries, will not please him."

"But we're not in Coronam," Jilly said. "So it's none of his business."

"Very true," Nurse Shannon agreed. "Beyond the Wall, what can he do?" A smile wreathed her freckled face, and she dug into her food.

Uncle Andrew looked at Anthea and raised one eyebrow. She nodded.

"We're still in Coronam," she said. "All the land is Coronam, north or south of the Wall."

"I've never understood it," Dr. Hewett said. "Could you explain, Miss Anthea?"

He was a quiet man who had once been a rider, but a bad

fall from a horse had shattered his right leg, and so he had gone to medical college in the south and returned to be the farm's doctor. Anthea had never exchanged more than a handful of words with him until he had helped her with Arthur, but he was staring at her now, waiting for an answer.

"If we're exiles," he continued, "doesn't that mean that we are beyond Coronam's borders?"

Anthea had never really thought about it. She blew her lips out, and caught Jilly's laughing face.

"Sorry," she said, blushing. "Too much time with Florian."

"Well, the Crown claims all the land from the Western Sea to the Ice Fields, which means that even though they call Leana the Exiled Lands, it's still part of Coronam."

"So there's no real exile?" Dr. Hewett said. "You just get sent . . . north?"

Anthea nodded. It sounded very foolish, saying it aloud.

"But even if we are still in Coronam, it's not illegal to keep horses," Jilly pointed out. "I looked it up once, and there's literally no law that says anything about horses."

"That's very true," Miss Ravel said. "The king may be unhappy about it, but legally we are free and clear."

"Do you think he cares about legalities? He can just change the law!" Perkins shook his head in disgust. "I'm sure it was the first thing he did!"

"We can just say that we have had horses since long before—" Finn began, but Perkins interrupted.

"Then they'll probably find some long-lost sacred tablet that says that horses are the devil's pets and we have to destroy them all or burn in hell!" he snapped.

"Language!" Nurse Shannon said.

She fluttered a hand toward one of Keth's ears, and he flinched away, blushing and looking to see if Jilly had noticed. Anthea caught Finn's eye and he blinked rapidly at her. She almost smiled, but then Caillin MacRennie picked up the letter, and any thought of smiling faded away.

"I want to know who *did* spill the beans," Caillin MacRennie put in. "That will tell us a great deal."

"I should think there was no question of that," Perkins said. "It's clear what happened, I'm only astonished it took her so long. That awful Cross woman ran out of secrets to feed her master, and so she finally blabbed. I just wonder how the witch covered her own tracks, since she's known about us so long."

Absolute silence greeted this.

Anthea was frozen with a forkful of roast beef halfway to her mouth. Looking across the table, she could see that Keth was, too. Her hand very slowly drifted down to the table, and she let her food slither off the fork to stain the clean white tablecloth. Nurse Shannon made another fluttering gesture as though wanting to cover Keth's ears again, and reach across the table to Anthea as well.

Blood rushed up Perkins's face until he was beet red. But he met Anthea's eyes steadily.

"I'm sorry, I should have been more . . . polite. But I stand by my statement: your mother is the one who told the king."

"Perkins," Uncle Andrew barked. "We don't know that!"

"Come now, man, why would she do it after all this time?" Caillin MacRennie argued.

"Does it even matter?" Jilly asked. "All that matters is that he knows."

Anthea stood up. Everyone fell silent.

"I wish to be excused," she said.

"Of course, Thea," her uncle said

All the men rose, but Anthea ignored them. Jilly started to get up, but Uncle Andrew shook his head at her. Anthea sailed out with as much dignity as she could muster and went to her room.

She stood in the middle of the floor for a while, not sure what to do with herself. Everyone at dinner had been certain that Anthea's mother had given the secret of Last Farm to the king. And they hated her for it.

What if they found out it was Anthea's fault? What if, for the first time, she had a family, but it was Anthea who ruined it?

WAITING

THE WORST PART WAS that nothing happened.

The king knew about Last Farm. People in the south, in Travertine, in the halls of the Royal Palace, knew there were horses alive and well. They must. If the king knew, he would make sure that everyone around him knew.

But nothing happened. There was no official letter from the king. There was no delegation from the south. There was only an unnerving silence.

Uncle Andrew was taking no chances. He had men riding along the outer fence, making sure that the tall stone structure was solid and kept out prying eyes. He had gone to the Wall, and had a long conversation with the small group of guards who were posted there. They all, as Anthea had suspected, looking back at her arrival, knew about the horses.

"You keep to yourselves, we keep to ourselves," the commander had told Uncle Andrew, and offered him a glass of whiskey.

And there were guns. Rifles. Pistols. All the men were trained to shoot, and now Anthea and Jilly were being shown how to use a pistol as well. Anthea felt sick the first time she had held a gun in her hand, but when her uncle had praised her as being a "natural shot," she had to admit she felt a little pride.

"We have to defend the horses," he had told her. "We can't let anyone hurt them."

"No," she had agreed, and learned how to brace her wrist without letting go of the reins.

But two weeks later, there was still nothing happening, and so things had relaxed a little. Enough for the young people to get permission to leave the farm and ride to the cliffs that overlooked the Bren Sea. The cliffs were riddled with holes where seabirds nested, and their raucous calls filled the air while the wind made a hollow music blasting through the holes that weren't filled with nests.

Anthea loved the sea. It was bottle green, with white-crested waves that looked like lace ruffles as they slapped the shore. She wanted to climb down and run along the sand, but Jilly told her not to even think about it until midsummer. The wind that fanned the waves was cold enough today to let her see the wisdom in that. She tried to do up the top button of her jacket, but Arthur complained. He was snuggled up with his beak and eyes just peering out between the lapels. She sighed; she would have to wear a scarf next time she rode.

Where the cliffs sloped down to meet the rocky shore was the village of Dorling-on-Sea. They weren't supposed to go there on horseback, even though the villagers were mostly Leanan, and probably knew about the farm, like the soldiers at the Wall.

Anthea looked longingly down the grass-covered slope to the village. There was a confectionary shop there that sold the most delectable marzipan she had ever tasted. The cook had had some brought in last week for Caillin MacRennie's birthday, and he had shared with them all at dinner.

"Are you sure we can't go down to the village?"

Just thinking about that marzipan, each piece shaped and painted like a tiny apple or peach, made her mouth water. She looked from Jilly to Finn, thinking that her cousin would certainly not mind some rule breaking, but Finn would probably stop them. Keth could go either way, she knew, depending on his mood.

"Thinking about marzipan?" Jilly's eyes gleamed.

"They have candied apples, too," Keth offered.

Finn wheeled his horse around so that he blocked the three of them.

"We are not going down into the village," Finn stated.

"You're no fun." Jilly pouted.

"*Your father* told us not to," Finn said.

"My father tells us a lot of things," Jilly countered, tossing her springy curls.

"Do you not care for the secrecy of the Last Farm?"

Jilly bristled, and spluttered, but finally subsided. She turned Buttercup around.

"Spoilsport," she muttered.

Anthea, however, did not turn Bluebell. "What secrecy?" she demanded. "We don't know who the king's told now!"

Finn's insistence that they follow Uncle Andrew's orders had stung her. She was the reason for it, she and her stupid letter, even if the others didn't know it.

"Hold," Finn said, reining in Marius.

They were on the hill that overlooked the farm now, and below them horses and men swarmed about in hectic patterns. Constantine was stamping and whinnying challenges, more so than usual.

"What is going on?" Keth said, squinting between his horse's ears. "Is that . . . a motorcar?"

"No. No. No," Anthea said.

"Goodness!" Jilly asked. "It *is* a motorcar! I've never seen one so modern!"

"I have," Anthea said flatly. "I've seen that one particularly."

They all looked at her.

"That's my uncle Daniel's car."

FLORIAN

Beloved Anthea was afraid.

Florian did not know who this man was, this Uncledaniel, but Florian hated him. He had come out of the silent, drowsy afternoon with his loud metal thing, his motorcar, and he had stood inside this motorcar and shouted for the men to attend him. Florian did not like the way he looked or talked or smelled, and then Beloved Anthea had come back on Bluebell. She was hiding in the paddock from Uncledaniel, and that compounded Florian's dislike.

Florian did not mind that Anthea was standing very close to him, using him as a shield between her and the house. He did not mind Bluebell standing close on her other side; together he and the mare would protect the Beloved.

He minded that she was so afraid.

He minded, too, when The Thornley came to the paddock fence, with anger in every line of his body, and demanded that Anthea leave Florian's side and go into the big house.

He minded that now she was more afraid than ever.

20

REUNION

"I SHOULD CHANGE," ANTHEA babbled as she trotted alongside Uncle Andrew. "Uncle Daniel is very proper . . . he's never seen . . . I'm still wearing . . ."

"He's never seen a horse before," Andrew said grimly. "I hardly think he will care what you are wearing, if he notices."

"Why did he . . . did he say . . ."

"He said he wanted to see you immediately, and that's all he would say."

Anthea was panting from the effort of keeping up with Uncle Andrew by the time they arrived in the dining room. The house had a lovely parlor, but Anthea supposed that there were too many people involved in this meeting to justify sitting in there. Also it felt less like a social call, more like a business meeting, Anthea reflected as she looked at the circle of expectant faces as they entered the room. Was that a good thing?

She supposed she would soon find out.

"There you are," Uncle Daniel said ungraciously as Anthea entered the dining room. "What in the name of all that's good are you wearing?"

Anthea had moved forward to kiss her uncle's cheek, but seeing him recoil from her, his eyes on her trousers, made her stop. Instead she walked, with burning cheeks, around the table to sit in an empty chair across from Uncle Daniel, next to Finn, who had all but run into the house as soon as they had reached the paddocks.

There was a twittering sound and a flutter inside her jacket, so she pulled out Arthur and set him on the arm of her chair. Dr. Hewett leaned around Finn and frowned at the rumpled state of the owl's feathers, and Anthea hurried to smooth them down. When she looked up, she saw that the expression of distaste Uncle Daniel had shown for her trousers was now extended to the owl.

"What is going on up here?" Uncle Daniel asked.

"The same thing that has been going on for decades," Uncle Andrew said coldly. "I have been looking after my family's estate. May I ask why *you* are here, and on the orders of the king?"

"Because the king did not know that you were committing treason!" Uncle Daniel shouted, rising to his feet.

Andrew had never sat down. He stood at the head of the table. He was much taller than Daniel, and his hands, gripping the wood of the chair in front of him, were brown and calloused and strong. Daniel saw all this at a glance and sat down again, though it did nothing to improve his mood.

"Kindly explain what you mean by treason," Uncle Andrew said with the tone of one who was about to lose his patience entirely.

"I mean this great compound, full of armed men, and horses, that's what I mean by treason," Daniel said in much the same tone.

"This? Compound?" Caillin MacRennie laughed. "This isnae a *compound*. It's just a farm! The Last Farm, we call it, since it holds the last of the horses in the world."

"And you say we are armed?" Uncle Andrew asked. "Is it considered treason to keep a few guns about, to shoot at foxes and the like that might get into our chicken coops?"

"Every man on this farm is carrying a pistol!"

"No, they aren't," Anthea said, wrinkling her nose. "First of all, you couldn't possibly have seen *every* man, and second, they . . . just aren't." She faltered as she saw the look on Uncle Daniel's face. "Sir?"

But Daniel wouldn't look at her now. His face had turned dark red with fury, and he was glaring at Andrew.

"You have had this girl here for what, a month? Two? And look at her!"

Anthea felt like she had been slapped. Finn took her hand and held it gently.

"She's brown as a farm laborer, wearing men's clothes, talking out of turn, carrying around wild animals—" He flicked his gaze to her, saw her holding Finn's hand, and added, "And fraternizing with strange boys!" As though that was the most horrible part of it all.

Anthea did not withdraw her hand from Finn's. With her other hand, she picked up Arthur and set him on her shoulder. He rubbed his round head against her cheek and she tilted her head to press against him.

"This was my father's work," she said. "I have no shame in continuing it."

Her uncle looked at her coldly. Then he took a folded piece of paper from his breast pocket. Anthea thought she might be sick.

"Then why did you write this letter?"

He threw it on the table so that everyone could see the signature. Anthea felt like all the blood was seeping out of her body, in sharp contrast to the continued red flush on Uncle Daniel's cheeks.

Finn let go of Anthea's hand. All eyes were either on the letter or on her, and Anthea herself didn't know where to look. There was no use in denying it, and she had no idea how to make it better.

The worst part was the expression on Uncle Andrew's face.

"It was when I first got here," Anthea said, her voice hardly more than a whisper. "Before!" She looked pleadingly at her uncle Andrew. "Before Florian."

He nodded, but his face didn't relax its grim lines.

"But the damage is done," Caillin MacRennie said.

"The damage? Hardly," Uncle Daniel said. "Reporting treason is not damaging."

"Tell me again how this is treason," Uncle Andrew said.

"Tell me how it isn't," Daniel fired back. "You are here, beyond the Wall, beyond the eye of the Crown, self-exiled, raising beasts that the Crown had destroyed—"

Finn let out a soft cry at that. Daniel stopped and gathered himself. Anthea wondered if he was supposed to say that. Her hands shook at the thought it might be true.

"You mean, we are caring for the last survivors of a plague that was accidentally spread to the people and horses of Leana . . . ? Isn't that what you meant to say?" Uncle Andrew goaded.

"And how is that treason?" Finn interjected. "Is it treason if you see a hurt . . . dog in the road and nurse it back to health?"

"It is if you lie to the Crown about the dog's existence," Daniel said.

"Did the Crown ever ask about the dog?" Andrew raised one eyebrow.

"Stop talking about a *dog*," Anthea choked out. "They're not dogs! They're horses! And, Uncle Daniel, they're wonderful!" She looked at him with hot, blurring eyes. "I have a horse named Florian, and he is . . . wonderful!" She couldn't think of any better word, any word that would do Florian justice.

Uncle Daniel made a disgusted noise.

Arthur suddenly hopped off her shoulder, walked into the middle of the table, and coughed up a pellet of bones and hair. It landed right on Anthea's incriminating letter. Everyone just stared for a moment.

Caillin MacRennie broke the silence by bursting out laughing a minute later.

"I feel the same, me," he said.

Anthea dared to raise her eyes, but then she saw Uncle Daniel's face. The tears blurring her eyes spilled over onto her cheeks, and she lurched to her feet, snatched up Arthur, and ran out the door.

She stumbled blindly across the yard to the paddock where she had left her horses. They were still there, although Bluebell had her tack off and even with tears running down her face, Anthea could tell that her frothy white mane had been carefully brushed.

"Thank you, Jilly," she bawled into Florian's shoulder.

"What's happening in there?" Jilly popped up from behind Buttercup. She was braiding her mare's tail as an excuse to loiter in the paddock nearest the house. "Is that really your uncle? Your *other* uncle, I mean? What's going on?"

"It's all my fault, Jilly," Anthea gasped out.

She set Arthur on top of Bluebell and used Florian's mane

to wipe her eyes. He sent her thoughts of love, and she sent them right back. Florian would love her no matter what, she knew. Even if no one else did, she would always have him.

Would she still have Jilly?

"Thea, dear, what is wrong?"

"Jilly," Anthea said. Her voice faltered. "Jilly, I love you. I wish I could be like you." She gestured to Jilly's purple silk scarf and black smoking jacket, and the effortless way her cousin was braiding Buttercup's tail without looking.

"I love you, too," Jilly said, bemused, "but—" Her eyes widened in horror. "Oh no! That awful other uncle isn't going to try and take you south, is he? Papa will put a stop to *that*." She looked like she was about to march into the house and give Uncle Daniel a piece of her mind.

"No, it's not that," Anthea said. "He . . . probably wants to, but nothing was said about it. It's just that, you see, it was me."

"What was you?" Jilly pulled a piece of ribbon out of her pocket and tied off the braid in Buttercup's tail without once taking her eyes off Anthea.

Anthea wanted to hide her face in Florian's mane again. But she knew she couldn't. She knew she had to face Jilly, of all people, when she said this. Instead she hooked her arm under his neck and brought his warm shoulder close to her, holding him tightly and feeling his love as she said the words.

"I'm the one who wrote the letter. I'm the one who told the king about Last Farm, and the horses."

21

Penance

"RUNNING AWAY?"

Jilly strolled into Anthea's room with Finn and Keth at her heels. She tucked the long pin she had used to pick Anthea's lock into the band of the jaunty bowler she wore perched atop her curls. All three of them looked at Anthea, packing her trunk, and then stood in a line between her and the door.

Anthea felt like a cornered fox. She had to force herself to turn her back on them and keep on shoving clothes into her trunk. It was clear that she couldn't stay here, with everyone hating her.

"Everyone except Florian," she said under her breath, and looked at the trunk in despair. Florian couldn't carry a trunk. What had she been thinking? She would need to find a knapsack or two and rig them to his saddle.

"Heading back to good ol' Travertine with dear Uncle

Daniel?" Jilly said, sitting down in Anthea's big chair. "I'm sure they will be delighted to have you. Little Batilda Rose—"

"It's *Belinda* Rose," Anthea said between gritted teeth, "and you know very well she hates me."

She blushed to say it, but it was true, and Jilly knew it. Anthea had confided in her . . . had told her everything about her old life. Anthea wondered, now, how much Jilly had told Finn. Had they laughed about her having to sleep on army cots crammed into attics, or having Belinda Rose pretend not to know her for her first month at Miss Miniver's? Anthea's face grew hot, and she stood hunched over her trunk, wrinkling a blouse in her clenched fists.

"Do you want to go back to Travertine?"

Finn sounded so gentle, and genuinely concerned, that Anthea dared to look up at him. He had a sharp crease between his brows, and his hands shoved deep in his pockets.

"Of course not," Anthea said. "I'm not packing to go with Uncle Daniel! I'm packing to . . . just . . . go."

"You could look up my mother. I'm sure she would have fun dressing you in sailor collars and taking you to parties," Jilly said.

"Jillian, stop that," Finn said, without looking at Jilly. His level blue eyes and Anthea's gray ones were still locked together. "Were you going to take Florian?"

"And Bluebell," Anthea admitted. "I suppose I'll have to just keep going north, live somewhere up by the Ice Fields."

"What were you going to do with that?" Keth indicated

her trunk, mostly with curiosity but also just a hint of derision. "Have Florian drag that giant trunk behind him like a
plow?"

"I don't know."

She closed the lid. She knew couldn't take the trunk. She
couldn't take anything with her but the bare necessities. And
what would they be? A blanket? Some clean underthings?
She had never slept outdoors before. A tent?

Jilly was humming, one leg over the arm of the chair. She
was trying to look devil-may-care, but Anthea knew that she was
deeply hurt. Anthea would never forget the expression of
betrayal on Jilly's face when she had told her about the letter.

"Is that why you're here?" Anthea said to Jilly. Her voice
was high and fast and she didn't sound like herself at all. "To
make sure I pack? To make sure I leave?"

Jilly leaped out of the chair as though she had been elec-
trocuted. "I'm not here to make sure you leave, I'm here to
make sure you fix this."

Another hot wave of tears ran down Anthea's cheeks. "But
I don't know how!" she wailed.

"There must be something," Keth said. "Can you reason
with your other uncle at all?"

"I doubt it," Anthea said, her voice barely more than a
whisper. "He wouldn't even look at the horses. Not Florian, not
even Bluebell. I just thought if he would only *meet* them . . ."

Her voice trailed off. She had a thought. A niggling, almost-
idea of a thought.

"That's always been the trouble," Finn agreed glumly. "I've always thought that if more people, more Coronami, had a chance to get to know our horses, they would be less hostile. But how do we get them to come past the Wall?"

"We don't," Anthea said, her idea taking shape. "We take the horses to them."

They all gaped at her. Jilly blinked a few times, closed her mouth, and then clapped softly. But Finn began to shake his head.

"Uncle Daniel wouldn't even walk across the yard to the fence," Anthea said. "There is no way you can get the king to leave Travertine and come all the way here. The king, or anyone else of influence."

"So we'll go to them," Jilly said, her face alight.

"No, I'll go," Anthea said. "I did this, I sent the letter, I need to make it right."

Her heart was pounding. She looked down at her trunk and shook her head. She would take only what she could fit in a saddlebag, and she would need to bring plenty of food for the horses. And how many of them could she take? Bluebell and Florian for certain, and perhaps two other mares?

"You can't take the whole herd to Travertine!" Keth said. He looked wild-eyed, and took a step toward the door.

"Stop," Finn ordered him. But then he turned to Anthea. "And you, you can't do this, either."

"I can and I will," Anthea said stubbornly.

"And so will I!" Jilly said.

Keth moaned and inched toward the door.

"Everyone stop for just a minute," Finn said. He was staring into space, his hands up around his face like he was about to cover his eyes.

"What if we gave him a horse, as a gift," Finn said at last.

"Who?" Keth asked.

"The king!" Jilly clapped her hands again. "King Gareth!"

Finn nodded. "You know how foreign rulers are always giving each other gifts? So that they stay friends and don't start wars?"

"Like the Kronenhofer emperor always giving King Gareth fine rugs and tapestries," Anthea said.

"Exactly!" Finn pointed at her in excitement. Arthur chose that moment to fly up from the desk and land on Finn's hand. Finn stroked the little owl as he continued to pace. "We take one of the stallions that doesn't have a rider to Travertine, and we give it to the king as a goodwill gift. That way everyone will know that horses are still alive, that they don't have diseases, *and* if King Gareth tries to get rid of it, he'll look like the villain. Kings aren't supposed to turn down gifts!"

Anthea was listening, but she wasn't looking at Finn. She was looking at the piece of paper that had slid across her desk when Arthur had launched himself at Finn. She began to shake her head slowly. The rest of her idea had blossomed in her brain.

"No, not the king," she said in a low voice.

"Definitely not," Jilly agreed. "That will make him think

that Finn is saying he's a king," Jilly said. "I mean, you are," she added, when they all looked at her. "But Gareth doesn't know that, and if he did, he'd be livid."

"She's right," Anthea said. She went to the desk. "You absolutely cannot give a horse to King Gareth. He would have both of you killed."

Finn deflated.

"However," Anthea went on, picking up the paper and unfolding it carefully. She traced the lower curve of the rose pressed into the wax. "If Jilly and I were to go to Bellair, with a few mares, that might be just the thing."

"Bellair?" Jilly said, puzzled.

"Mares?" Finn said. "Why?"

Anthea held up the letter so that they could see the signature. Keth whistled.

"Why, for the queen and the princesses, of course."

FLORIAN

Florian was filled with excitement. He did not know what Beloved Anthea was doing in the stable at night, with the Soon King, She Who Was Jilly, and the Leggy Boy, but as it included him, he did not mind at all.

They were saddling a small herd of horses, and the Soon King was giving strict instructions on feeding and watering. He was not saddling Marius, or even making a move toward Constantine's end of the stable. Instead, the Soon King was filling bags and tying them to mares.

"My darling," Beloved Anthea whispered in his ear as she began to tie bags of oats across his saddle. "Can you be so quiet for me? Can you be so brave? Will you mind Keth's Gaius Julius, and let him be the herd stallion for this journey?"

The Soon King, hearing this as he handed her another bag,

began to shake his head. "It is not a good idea to take so many stallions."

"I will never leave Last Farm again without my Florian," Beloved Anthea said sharply. "I promised." Thoughts of love and reassurance came to him. She would take him, no matter what the Soon King said.

"He's not the one I worry about," the Soon King said, leaning in close. "Caesar? Leonidas?"

Florian shivered. Caesar was a good, strong animal, a loyal companion. Leonidas was full of pride, and did not trust any man. He had only rarely been ridden.

"Jilly is refusing to go without Caesar," Beloved Anthea whispered. "She is always asking to ride him. And he seems to like her well enough."

"No. Riding. Stallions." The Soon King sounded terrified.

"Yes, *Uncle*," Beloved Anthea said. "And Keth seems confident enough about Leonidas."

"I hope so."

"I want to take Blossom and Minty," She Who Was Jilly called down the aisle.

"No!" Beloved Anthea stuck her head over the door of Florian's stall.

The Soon King unlatched it for her and she led him out as she shook her head at She Who Was Jilly. Florian was glad. It was not proper that they take a mare in foal out in the night, and his Beloved said as much.

"Oh, I didn't realize," She Who Was Jilly said. "But what about Blossom?"

Again Beloved Anthea shook her head. "Bluebell hates her," she whispered.

So it was that the sisters, Juniper and Holly, joined Campanula, Bluebell, Buttercup, Caesar, Leonidas, and Florian in the darkness behind the stable. They were attached by long leads, and heavily laden with bags of fodder plus food and other goods for the humans.

"This is a terrible idea," the Leggy Boy said.

"It will work," the Soon King said. "I'll go rouse Constantine. When he starts, you run."

Florian did not like this. Not one bit. Beloved Anthea had just mounted Bluebell, and he heard her sharp intake of breath. He nudged her knee with his nose, to let her know that he agreed.

"What are you going to do?" Beloved Anthea asked him. "How will you—"

"At least let me do this," the Soon King said with anger. "I cannot go with you, but I can keep them from following you."

Waves of fear came from Beloved Anthea. But she rubbed Florian's neck as she guided Bluebell toward the gate. Because of Uncledaniel there was a rider standing guard there, which is why the Soon King and Constantine needed to draw attention away.

They waited in the shadows. Beloved Anthea did her best to soothe all the mares and stallions. Gaius Julius was being fractious, and so the Leggy Boy passed the lead to Leonidas and two of the mares to She Who Was Jilly to hold while he tried to settle his mount.

Then came the scream of the herd stallion. Then came the stampede of his hooves out of the stable, toward the Big House, with the Soon King running behind and shouting.

Gaius Julius reared, screaming. The Leggy Boy fell from his back and let out a scream of his own, one of pain. Gaius Julius bolted for the safety of the stable.

"My arm," the Leggy Boy screamed. "It's broken!"

"Jilly, go!" Beloved Anthea cried, and she kicked Bluebell's sides.

Florian stayed close to his Beloved, pulling the uncertain mares behind him, as she and Bluebell led them down the long drive, past the confused rider at the gate, and out of Last Farm.

He did not know where they were going, but he had faith that his Beloved Anthea would guide them all to safety.

22

PEACE MISSION

"I DIDN'T THINK THIS would be so boring," Jilly announced as they clopped down the road.

"It can't all be wild midnight chases," Anthea said.

"But that was so much fun," Jilly said, her eyes lighting up at the memory.

Anthea shuddered. As they had swept out of the gates of Last Farm, Anthea had been sure that the startled sentries would shoot at them. When that failed to happen, and when the strings of horses they were leading had realized that Finn was not with them and that back at the farm their herd stallion was having a fit, they had all tried to stop at once.

While Jilly had kept spurring on Buttercup, calling out for them to follow her, Anthea had brought up the rear. She had broken out in a sweat trying to send a great cloud of encouragement to all the horses with them.

Please keep running, please keep running, she had chanted over and over in her head.

The mares had only hesitated a moment, but then they had agreed with her and kept going. Florian, of course, had stayed right beside Bluebell and never wavered. Leonidas had balked, and Anthea had had to grab hold of his bridle with one hand and drag him.

Keep running, you!

He had been so startled by this that he had put on a burst of speed. But now that they were south of the Wall, he seemed to delight in dragging his heels and sending prickly, sullen thoughts to Anthea, who largely ignored them.

"Can't we do another run?" Jilly said now. "Recapture some of that magical excitement?"

"We have a long way to go," Anthea reminded her.

Jilly blew out her lips in a gesture not unlike the one Buttercup had just made

"I thought this would all be much more *urgent*," Jilly said. "Galloping over the hills, up at dawn, riding until midnight." She twitched the reins, moving Buttercup to a faster walk.

"This mission *is* urgent," Anthea said. Bluebell, sensing her irritation, flicked an ear and quickstepped a little. Anthea let her move forward until they were abreast of Jilly and Buttercup. "But we can hardly gallop the horses night and day to get there. They'd drop dead of exhaustion." She lowered her voice on that last sentence, but Bluebell flicked her ears nervously all the same.

"Yes, but must there be so many *trees*? If all these trees weren't here, the road wouldn't wind so, and we could—"

"Jilly. Dear." Anthea interrupted her cousin's rant before she became unstoppable. "It's a *forest*. It has to have trees."

Jilly subsided.

They had been on the road for two days. In that time they had not seen one single soul, something that put both of them on edge. Jilly reacted by becoming even chattier and more flippant, and Anthea responded with . . . well, she didn't really know how she was responding, but she was sure it wasn't well. She was so tense that she felt like a twisted cord ran between her shoulder blades and kept getting tighter and tighter. The horses flinched whenever she spoke.

Florian sped up a little so that he was closer to Bluebell, bumping affectionately against Anthea's foot. Campanula, one of the other horses Anthea was leading, tried to slow down instead. She was normally a docile enough beast, but the girls' nerves were affecting her very strongly, and she was becoming stubborn or fractious by turns, behavior normally expected from Leonidas, but not from one of the mares. Anthea wondered if Campanula was a good choice for a gift to the queen, but it was too late now.

"Come along," Anthea said as brightly as she could manage.

Anthea tugged at Campanula's lead. She got an impression of the mare lying down in the middle of the road, and gave the lead another tug.

"Don't you dare, you foolish thing," she snapped. "I'll have Florian drag you!"

Campanula gave a sneering whinny, so Anthea turned in her saddle to make eye contact.

"Just try me," she said in a low voice.

With a toss of her mane, Campanula sped up. Anthea tried to ignore her as she thought about Finn.

She did not want to think about Finn, but she knew she would have to stop avoiding the issue at some point. Better to do it now, when he was nowhere near, and firm up her resolve. Prior to their leaving, Finn had done something . . . alarming.

Anthea had been alone in her room again, packing her saddlebags, when he had knocked on her door. Assuming it was Jilly, she had called out for her cousin to enter. But when she turned around Finn was standing on her rug.

"Try not to let Jilly get you killed," he'd said, and held out a small box.

Anthea stepped forward and took it from him, still unable to come up with an answer. It was a silver horseshoe pendant on a fine chain, like the one Caillin MacRennie wore. Jilly had one, too. Her mouth opened and then closed, and she looked up at him, wondering where he had gotten it.

"I was saving it for your birthday," he had said. "I mean, it used to be yours. The charm. Your father gave it to you. But it was on a horsehair cord. I got the chain for you. But I thought you should have it now." He was blushing dark red.

Before she could thank him, he had kissed her on the cheek and then fled. Anthea had been left holding the box in one hand, her other hand pressed to her cheek.

Anthea had thought about asking Jilly for advice, but only for a moment. Jilly would probably just tell Anthea to go ahead and kiss him back!

And then there was the matter of the jewelry. Manners dictated that a young lady not accept gifts from a young man. But handing it back seemed . . . ungracious . . . as well as awkward. And the charm was hers, after all. She had put the necklace on, had not taken it off since, but was wearing it tucked under her clothes.

Sensing her thoughts about Finn, Florian sent her a welter of images: the stables, Finn bringing him sugar, all of them at the farm, happy and safe.

"Yes, yes," she muttered under her breath. "I know what *you'd* advise."

Florian drooped, and Bluebell threw up her head and let out a protesting whinny. Anthea quickly stroked their necks, assuring them that they were her favorites.

It had been a very nice kiss, she had to admit once the horses were calmed. His lips had been very warm and soft.

Up ahead, Jilly was singing—or rather, chanting—some Leanan ballad. Anthea settled into her saddle. Leanan ballads always began with the hero's lineage, then the lineage of everyone else mentioned in the course of the song, before they ever got to the hero's deeds. It would keep Jilly entertained for an hour or more.

When Jilly came to the chorus, since Anthea had heard this ballad several times from the riders, Anthea threw back her head and joined in. Campanula shied and Jilly stopped singing to let out an oath. Then she grinned at Anthea and continued to sing. Bluebell, who had sensed what Anthea was going to do, shook her head and snorted, but made no further comment.

They trotted on down the road, roaring out the rest of the ballad, and then another and another, until it was nearly time to make camp for the night. The sky was just growing dark, and Anthea noticed that the horses' thirst was starting to bother her as well. She called ahead to Jilly mid-song, and the other girl nodded without stopping. Anthea had just taken a breath and was about to rejoin the chorus when a man stepped out of the trees to their right.

The mares on the leads all shied, and Jilly swore, while Florian half reared and then lunged at the man, pulling Bluebell along in his wake. With Constantine miles behind them, Anthea had told him that the mares were his responsibility.

"Florian, no! Get back!" She yanked on the lead, trying to keep him from trampling the man. She made a mental note to put his lead on a slipknot in the future.

Now that they were all turned, facing the stranger, Anthea could see that he hadn't just popped out of the woods but had instead come along a narrow road that cut through the trees and led off to the south and west. He looked to be in his forties, with graying brown hair and a thick wool jacket that spoke of prosperity even as it screamed out its rusticity.

"Ho, there! Control your beasts!" The man raised both his hands to show they were empty.

"Don't leap out and scare them, then," Anthea snapped.

Jilly snorted and gave Anthea a half-amused, half-shocked look.

"I mean," Anthea said, recovering. "I beg your pardon, sir?"

"What are they—who are you?" he stammered.

"We have just come from Leana," Jilly said with a winning smile. "We are on our way south to meet with Her Majesty, Queen Josephine, and give her the gift of these magnificent horses."

The man goggled. Anthea hissed. Jilly just beamed.

"Would you like to pet one?" Jilly asked. "They're quite tame."

"They're supposed to be *dead*," the man said in disbelief.

"That's a common misconception," Jilly said, in an excellent imitation of Miss Ravel. "They were all taken beyond the Wall to keep them safe, because they were at *risk* from plague, and not because they *caused* plague.

"But now the queen has asked to learn to ride, so we're bringing her some fine mares," Jilly embroidered.

Anthea almost made another hissing noise, wanting her

cousin to quit before she dug in too deep. But she didn't want to upset the horses, or the man, so instead she pasted on a bright smile.

"Now, now, I'm sure the good gentleman is quite busy," Anthea said. "But, we are on the road to Bellair, are we not?" She let out a tinkling laugh. "I must confess: I'm dreadful with maps!"

"Are you . . . are you Rose Candidates?" The man had looked at Anthea, and his eyes had snagged on the silver pendant she wore prominently pinned to the lapel of her jacket.

"I attended Miss Miniver's Rose Academy in Travertine," Anthea said, relieved that she didn't have to make up a lie.

"Are there are a lot of horses in . . . Leana?" the man asked.

"There are some," Anthea said vaguely.

"I didn't know that," the man said. "Or that it was still called Leana." He edged a little closer to Buttercup.

"There are, and it is," Jilly said winningly.

"This is the right road, by the way," the man said, looking Buttercup up and down with wondering eyes. "Well, it's one of them. I think the Blackham Road would take you there more straightly. This is just an old country road, it's going to swing you wide around the forest."

"Ah, yes," Anthea said, ignoring Jilly's pointed look. "That's what we thought. Better for the horses to avoid running afoul of motorcars, though." She directed this last at Jilly, who knew very well why they were taking the "boring" road through the forest.

"Don't know too many farmers that can afford a motorcar," the man agreed. "This is oxcart country."

Then, greatly daring, he held out a hand. Buttercup put her soft nose into his palm, then shook her head in disgust when it turned out that the man didn't have any sugar or apples to offer her. The man leaped back at her quick motion, but then he laughed.

"Well, now!" he said. "There was a thing to tell the kiddies when I get home!"

"Where are you going?" Anthea asked. She wondered if they ought to offer him a ride, or at least to walk alongside them, for the sake of more good public relations.

"Tillbury," he said, and pointed back the way they had come. Then he jerked a thumb at the little side lane he had just come from. "There's a few farms down thataway. I go twice a month to see if anyone needs doctoring. I'm the only physician hereabouts," he added by way of explanation.

He reached out a hand toward Leonidas, who condescended to lip at his fingers. The man chuckled at the way it tickled.

"We had best be off," Jilly said. "Mustn't keep Her Majesty waiting!"

Anthea cringed, but the man didn't notice. Anthea and Jilly turned the horses to start back along the road, and the man stepped back. Before they rode away, however, Anthea had to ask one question.

"Aren't you afraid?"

"Afraid?" He looked along the road. "There's blessed few bandits in these parts, miss."

"No," Anthea said. "I meant, aren't you afraid of the horses?"

He shook his head. "Like I said, I'm a physician." He looked Anthea squarely in the eyes. "I know all about disease and plagues." He patted Bluebell's neck and then waved to Jilly.

Once they were out of earshot Jilly began her ballad again, but Anthea didn't join this time. Her cousin started another, one Anthea didn't know, and she listened with half an ear as she thought about the man. He was the first honest-to-goodness Coronami who had seen a horse, and he hadn't cared one whit. In fact, he had seemed excited by the horses. But would everyone be as excited? And what if their fears about the king came true, and he declared them all traitors?

What if this mission failed?

Sensing her pensiveness, Florian moved in close and bumped her foot with his shoulder again. Thoughts of warm oat mash and love blanketed her, and she gave a little laugh, feeling some of the tension between her shoulders unwind. They had been seen by a regular citizen, and it had all turned out all right.

"My love, my love, do not forsake me," Jilly sang.

"So dramatic," Anthea whispered to Bluebell's mane, rolling her eyes. She reached over and tweaked Florian's ear. "My love, my love, do not forsake me."

Florian nodded his head.

23

FASTER AND FASTER...

"I HAVE EXCELLENT NEWS," Anthea announced two days later. She was holding a map up as though reading a newspaper, the pencil that she had used to trace their route tucked behind her ear.

"You're going to bank the fire?" Jilly said.

She was just wiping off their frying pan after making them breakfast, and stowing their tin plates and mugs in her saddlebags. She had been camping before, with her father, and knew how to cook over a fire, much to Anthea's surprise. The only thing that Anthea could make without burning it was toast, and even that was sometimes a dodgy prospect.

She did enjoy making fires, and putting them out, however.

"Yes, I will," Anthea said absently. "But I have better news."

She laid the map flat on the fallen log they had used as a bench, and made an *X* with her pencil.

"We are here," she said grandly. Then she pointed to a mark a few inches away. "And that is Bell Hyde." She put a lopsided circle around it.

"And that's Bellair," Jilly said, looking over her shoulder and sighing. "Even farther down the road."

"But we're not actually going to Bellair," Anthea told her. "We're going to Bell Hyde."

"Wait, we are? Why?"

"Because Bell Hyde is the name of the queen's favorite estate, and where she spends every summer with the princesses and her Favored Rose Maidens," Anthea said. "If the court is on schedule, and they have not changed the schedule in decades, then they have been in residence there for two weeks."

"That's why we're going toward Bellair, not Travertine," Jilly said. She mimed hitting herself on the head with the heavy pan.

"Yes," Anthea said, then she frowned. "If you didn't know why we were going this way, why didn't you ask before?"

"I was afraid of looking stupid," Jilly said with a shrug.

Anthea shook her head over that. "Anyway," she continued. "We should be able to reach Bell Hyde in two days, three at the most." She folded up the map. "The only trouble will be people," she said quietly.

"What was that?" Jilly had been fussing with her saddle-bags, and now she turned around, flushed from yanking on them to make sure they were hanging evenly.

"I said we have to watch out for people now," Anthea said. "We're still in the countryside, but we're in the part of the countryside with all the estates, and motorcars."

"And the Coronami?" Jilly asked.

"And the Coronami," Anthea said.

Jilly looked like she was going to say something else, but she changed her mind and finished packing. Anthea was glad. She didn't know when she had started to think of the Coronami as . . . the Coronami. Or when, in her head, she had started to call herself a Leanan, but she did know she wasn't ready to talk about it yet.

"And my father," Jilly said, grimacing.

"I hate asking someone to lie," Anthea said, "but in this case—"

"We just have to hope that Finn lied his face off," Jilly agreed.

"Yes," Anthea said with a sigh. "I feel so guilty sending your father to Travertine to look for us, but it gives us more time!"

"Finn is good at . . . well, not so much lying as not saying the whole truth," Jilly said. "I've always thought it made him seem very royal."

"We can only hope," Anthea said. "But let's not dawdle, all the same!"

She shoveled dirt over their fire and tied her small hand shovel to Leonidas's baggage.

"On to the queen!" Jilly cheered as she mounted.

Anthea wished she could feel so excited. Instead she just felt *gritty*. Sleeping on the ground, washing up in streams, eating over a smoky fire . . . It was hardly glamorous. It was, in fact, merely hard. Every part of Anthea was sore, from the rocks on the ground and the long days in the saddle. Even her brain was sore, from wrestling with the horses.

Florian, naturally, kept her buoyed up with his thoughts of love. And Bluebell was also being refreshingly obedient, though Anthea's nervousness made her nervous as well. But Anthea felt like she was being worn thin, like a linen shirt that had been laundered too many times. By the time they got to Bell Hyde, filthy and exhausted, she wondered if she would simply fall in a faint at the queen's feet.

If they managed to get an audience with the queen at all.

"What were we thinking?" Anthea said aloud as they started down the road. "Why are we doing this alone?"

Jilly, her mouth open to begin yet another ballad, closed it. But then she shrugged and opened her mouth again to answer.

"It was your idea," she reminded Anthea, but not in an accusatory way. "And it was a good idea."

"Was it?"

"Yes," Jilly said decisively. "Even if your hunch about the

queen is wrong, from her letter she seems much more kindly and sensible than her husband. Surely she will see reason."

Anthea just nodded, more in hope than in agreement. She hauled on the lead line tied to the left side of her saddle. Leonidas was on that line, with two mares, Holly and Juniper, tied to him. On her right she kept Florian, and after the encounter with the physician from Tillbury, she had Florian's lead on a slipknot. Jilly had Caesar tied to her saddle, with Campanula trailing him.

"I feel like this is going to turn bad," Anthea muttered. "Soon."

"Don't look for rain clouds, if there's no rain," Jilly sang.

Anthea squinted at the sky. And now she was worried about the weather turning bad, as well as a myriad of other things. Running out of feed. The horses being spooked by a motorcar. Soldiers cropping up out of a hedgerow and mistaking them for enemy invaders.

There were, she realized, hedgerows now. They had come out of the seemingly endless forest and were starting to see fields bordered by low stone fences or tall hedges, though there were only distant signs of people. Anthea felt all her sore muscles clench.

Bluebell moved into a trot, and the others followed. Florian whinnied, and bumped his shoulder against Anthea's boot a few times. Jilly gave a small *whoop* and let Buttercup have her head. They hadn't had a gallop yet that day, anyway, so Anthea went along with it. She hated to admit, even to herself, that it was just her own nerves causing her horses to speed up.

She did love the feeling of the wind in her hair. They had been plodding for too long. The ribbon holding her hair back started to come loose, and she reached around and grabbed it, stuffing it into a pocket as she gave Bluebell her head. The horses went faster and faster. The horses were also happy to gallop; their feelings of freedom and joy rushed to Anthea's heart as they picked up the pace.

Assuming that Finn had managed to send any search party toward Travertine, they would make it to Bell Hyde long before her uncle found out they were not with the king. But still, they weren't sure if Andrew had gotten the truth out of Finn. So they had either a three-day head start, or a two-hour head start. She dug her heels into Bluebell and chirruped to the other horses.

And faster and faster.

Anthea thought of her first riding lesson. She remembered Bluebell going round and round and not stopping when she was told. Leonidas had just passed Bluebell and was straining at the end of his lead a length ahead of her.

And faster and faster.

All Anthea could hear was the clatter of their hooves on the hard road. All she could see was the high hedgerow on either side. She only noticed the break in the hedgerow right as Leonidas and Buttercup reached it, and she felt their feelings shift from complete joy to utter fear.

A tractor, belching black smoke and ridden by a large farmer, came rumbling out of the field. Jilly managed to swerve Buttercup, letting out a curse, but Caesar ran afoul of its front end. He screamed and reared and then fell heavily onto his side, his tightly tied lead dragging Jilly's saddle awry so that she crashed down atop him.

All the horses screamed and panicked. Florian slipped his lead free and turned on the tractor, rearing back and letting out a war cry. The farmer, face white beneath his tan and eyes wild, bailed sideways off his seat and let the tractor keep rolling down the road. It ran into another hedge and stopped with a crunch: there was a stone fence on the other side of the greenery.

Anthea sat back hard and told Bluebell *whoa* in her mind, making the word lash like a whip. Bluebell almost landed on her haunches, she stopped so fast, but Anthea was ready for it and didn't fly out of the saddle this time.

She did leap, safely, off Bluebell's back once the horse had stopped and went at once to Jilly. Her cousin had rolled free of the thrashing legs of the horses, her hands tucked around her head as they had had been taught. Anthea grabbed her arm and helped her up and then immediately grabbed Caesar's bridle.

The big red stallion was still on his side, screaming and thrashing. He had a gash on his shoulder and scrapes on his legs, but to Anthea's relief she could not see any broken bones. She was shaking with fear, but all the same she looked him in the eye and firmly told him to calm down and get up.

Caesar just lay there, trembling.

"Listen to me, you silly creature," Anthea snapped, trying to cover her fear with anger. "I told them to get that sponge out of your throat. Now I'm telling you to get up."

Caesar got up.

Jilly had sensibly grabbed the reins of Buttercup and Bluebell, though she herself was standing with one foot barely touching the ground. Bluebell's saddle was hanging around her belly, and her saddlebags were almost touching the ground. The mares were whinnying and stamping, tugging at their leads.

Florian, however, was standing very still in the middle of it all. He whickered softly and touched the mares within his reach on the neck with his nose, calming them. Anthea's heart filled with love for him, and she turned a little of that toward Caesar to help soothe him.

"Are you hurt?" Anthea asked her cousin.

"Just bruised," Jilly said. "Maybe twisted my knee. How's Caesar?"

Anthea looked at his shoulder. It wasn't as bad as she had thought. She relaxed even more and rubbed his face, trying to radiate calm.

"Those are horses," the farmer said. He was absently dusting off the seat of his canvas trousers over and over again. "Those are *horses*," he said again, as though Jilly and Anthea were unaware.

"Yes, they are," Jilly said, with considerably less graciousness than she had shown to the last man they had met on the road.

"Are you hurt, sir?" Anthea asked, remembering her manners.

Her eyes, however, were on Caesar's shoulder. His wound wasn't deep, but it would need to be stitched.

"I'm not, but my tractor—" He broke off as he saw his tractor across the lane, still whirring and grinding as it tried to plow through the stone wall. "My tractor!"

He ran over to turn off the engine.

Anthea continued to calm Caesar, wondering if the farmer could help them find a surgeon who might stitch up a horse. She had to push Florian and Bluebell away, gently, as they kept nudging her with their noses. She didn't look up until Jilly said her name, very loudly, with a swear word coming right after.

"What's wrong?" Anthea said.

The farmer was heading back to them, having apparently given up his tractor as a loss, at least for now. He was giving the horses a bemused but not hostile look, and they in turn—

"Jilly!" Anthea said sharply, looking over their charges. "Where are Leonidas and Holly and Juniper?"

"I've been trying to tell you," Jilly said. "I don't know! They're just gone!"

24

HUNTING PARTY

"THEY MUST HAVE BOLTED," Jilly said.

"Correction," Anthea said grimly, "*Leonidas* bolted, and he took the mares with him."

"They went that way," the farmer said, pointing into the field he had just come from on his tractor. "While I was lyin' there one of 'em almost stepped on me."

"I'm sorry," Anthea said, feeling numb. "I'm sorry. But you're all right? You're all right."

"What should we do?" Jilly said. She reached out a hand and let Caesar nuzzle her palm. She couldn't see his injury from the side she was on. "Is he all right?"

Anthea turned him so that Jilly and the farmer could see. The man let out a low whistle and Jilly gasped.

"He needs a surgeon," Anthea said. She gave the reins to

Jilly. "You need to get Buttercup's saddle right, and find a place to rest."

"You are welcome to bring them to my barn," the farmer said. Then he stopped and his brow wrinkled. "Are they . . . sickly?"

"No," Anthea said. "They don't have any diseases."

The farmer nodded. "Could a man used to doctoring oxen and cattle take care of that one?" He pointed to Caesar.

"Yes!" Jilly almost shouted in excitement, making the man jump and Buttercup flinch.

"Good," Anthea said.

She took Bluebell's reins from Jilly, who got a better grip on Caesar. Anthea unclipped the lead line from Florian and stuck it in a saddlebag. He wore a saddle, with heavy panniers on each side that were now half-empty of food and fodder. She took those off and left them sitting in the road, then made sure that the reins knotted at his neck wouldn't come loose and tangle in his front legs.

"What are you doing?" Jilly asked as Anthea swung into Bluebell's saddle.

"I need you to take the others," Anthea said. She wished that she had more time to celebrate the fact that she had just gotten so gracefully into the saddle without a mounting block, but unfortunately she didn't. "Take care of Caesar, rest."

Anthea stopped. She closed her eyes for just a moment and breathed deeply. Her hair itched. Her eyes felt sandy.

"Jilly," she said as she opened her eyes, "if I'm not back by tomorrow night, keep going down the road to Bell Hyde." She pulled the map out of her saddlebag and tossed it to Jilly.

Jilly didn't catch it. It flapped to the ground at her feet while she stared at Anthea. "What are you going to do?" she asked again. "Anthea?"

"One of us has to get to Bell Hyde. One of us has to convince the queen that the horses need her protection," Anthea said.

"But I don't—"

"The horses love you," Anthea interrupted her cousin. She felt a smile break out across her face. "Buttercup and Caesar especially. They know you. And you have been riding since before you could walk. You can do this, Jilly. You have to.

"Because I have to go after the mares and Leonidas, and when I find him, I'm going to pull him back to the road by. His. Tail."

She kicked her heels into Bluebell's sides. Florian strode alongside them. They left Jilly and the farmer and the other horses behind and headed between the high hedges.

There were rolling green fields ahead of them. They could see the marks of the tractor's heavy wheels in the hard-packed dirt that rimmed the edge of the field. And going in a diagonal across it, trampling the tender shoots of whatever crop had been sown here, were hoofprints. Leonidas and the mares had gone through the hedge and straight out the opposite corner of the field. Anthea could see the ravaged hedge, and to her even greater despair, a copse of trees on the far side.

"Stupid forest! Why are there so many trees?" she muttered, finally agreeing with Jilly about the trees. She had Bluebell and Florian walk single file along the edge of the field, so that they didn't do any further damage.

Once through the hedge, they found themselves in a dense copse, or possibly a last offshoot of the northern forest. There was no sign of the three missing horses.

Anthea tried to reach out to them, tried to feel their minds as Caillin MacRennie had taught her. But all she could feel was that she was scared, and more than a little angry at Leonidas for not staying with her.

She looked at Florian.

"Find them," she said. "I-I can't."

Florian stepped in front of Bluebell and then he stretched his neck out and bugled. There was no other word for it: he bugled a call that made Anthea want to move closer to him, and Bluebell, too, stepping over until she was close beside the stallion without any urging.

They all three waited, hardly breathing, and then there was an answering call, followed by the sound of hooves crushing the leaves that littered the forest floor. Florian called again, and again was answered, and the sound of horses became more frantic.

Holly, a black mare with a white mark on her forehead

shaped like a sprig of holly, burst through the trees with Juniper, a rich chestnut-colored mare, behind her. They clustered around Florian and Bluebell, whickering, bumping shoulders, shaking manes, nipping fondly at each other.

"Good girls, good girls," Anthea chanted

They had twigs and leaves in their manes and tails, and the lead that had tied Holly to Leonidas had broken off short and wrapped around one of her legs. Anthea's relief at seeing them, uninjured, cleared up her mind and she was able to welcome them through the Way as well as by stroking their necks and plucking some of the twigs out.

They waited just a minute, Anthea and Florian, and then Florian's head came up and his ears went back. She felt a pulling on the sides of her head as though her ears had tried to do the same.

"Leonidas!" Anthea's voice cracked as she shouted. "Leonidas! Come!"

She wondered if he would be offended at being called like a dog, but then perhaps his indignation would make him come faster. But there was no sound of hoofbeats coming through the wood, no crackle of leaves and branches. She thought she could sense him, but she wasn't sure. How far away was he?

"Juniper," she said, grabbing the bridle of the mare hovering by her right knee. "Where is Leonidas?"

Her head throbbed as she tried to use the Way to gather up

Juniper's scattered thoughts. She'd never tried so hard to communicate with a horse other than Bluebell or Florian before.

"All of you, be quiet," she ordered.

Her stern tone made the mares even more jittery, and Florian stiffened, offended. Juniper pulled her bridle out of Anthea's grip, but she snatched it back.

"Now, now, I'm sorry," she soothed. "But we have to find Leonidas. Where is he?" She gazed deeply into Juniper's eyes, and she snorted.

Scratching, pricking, burning. Anthea could feel it in her own mind as well, now that she was calmer and had seen that the mares were safe.

Brambles. He was caught in some brambles.

"Take us to Leonidas," Anthea said, as gently as she could manage. "Please, Juniper darling?"

Juniper snorted again, but she wheeled and led them back into the woods. Holly hesitated, but Florian nudged her and they all trailed after Juniper, Anthea and Bluebell bringing up the rear.

It was a matter of minutes to find Leonidas, but when they did, Anthea drooped in despair. Juniper hadn't understood what had happened to the runaway stallion, but Anthea understood very well.

Leonidas wasn't caught in brambles, he was caught in a snare used for wolves or deer. A cat's cradle strung between two trees, low to the ground, so that any segment the animal stepped in, no matter how delicately, caused the whole trap to tighten on its leg. Not only were both of Leonidas's front legs wrapped with the fine wires of the snare, but his reins had gotten knotted into them as well.

Anthea had a clasp knife in her saddlebags, with a blade as long as her middle finger. It was wickedly sharp, and would do the job, but it would require her to climb around the legs of a large stallion whose mind was a moil of pain and panic.

She looked at the snare, and then at Leonidas. He looked at her. Florian nuzzled her arm, and she felt hope from him. No, not hope: certainty. Anthea would fix it, Florian knew. In his mind, she could fix anything.

"I hope Leonidas agrees," she muttered.

At the sound of her voice Leonidas shifted, and the wires cut into his left foreleg even more. He neighed, pleading. His huge round eyes looked at her, waiting for her to make it all right.

"Okay," she told him. "I will, I will help you. Then we will find Jilly, okay?"

Leonidas threw his head up and down, nodding.

Anthea closed her eyes, bracing herself. *You must all be calm. Calm and still*, she thought to them. She opened her eyes.

And saw Arthur staring at her from over Leonidas's shoulder. She gaped at the owl. He gave a pleased hoot in reply.

"I left you at home," she said in astonishment.

He hooted again.

"All right," she said. "It's no use arguing, I suppose. Let's get Leonidas free."

The problem of getting Leonidas free was not falling into the snare herself. She picked her way carefully over and around the snare, feeling sweat trickle down her spine, while the horses and Arthur watched. When she reached the first of the wires that were entangling Leonidas, she gingerly squatted on her heels. She opened the knife, gripped the wire in one hand, and hacked it with her shining, never-before-used blade.

With a twang the wire parted and whipped around. The end she held in her left hand slipped through her fingers so rapidly that she was glad she wore gloves, otherwise it would have sliced right through her fingers. As it was, the leather of her gloves was cut, but not all the way through, fortunately.

Cutting that one wire had released the tension of the snare, and now she could climb over the slack wires to Leonidas, who sighed with relief. His legs were still hopelessly entangled, but it would be only a matter of minutes to get him free.

But you must hold still.

He snorted. It was better than nothing, coming from Leonidas.

Anthea sawed at the wires. It was much harder when they were slack. She had to pull them tight so that there was tension against the knife, but without cutting Leonidas. One of them was still wound so tightly around his left foreleg that when she tried to pull it taut to cut it, it sliced right into the muscle.

Leonidas screamed and reared. The wires that were still wrapped around his legs arced through the air with a singing noise. Anthea was sure she would hear that sound in her nightmares for years to come. A wire slashed open her face just below the left eyebrow, narrowly missing her eye, and a rivulet of blood obscured her vision. Dimly, Anthea heard Florian and Bluebell both scream in pain as well. She herself was too shocked to make a sound.

Leonidas freed himself and bolted deeper into the woods, frightened and in pain, trailing wires from his lacerated legs. The other horses stirred hectically, whickering and neighing with nerves, trampling the bushes, and risking further entrapment.

Anthea lurched to a standing position. She couldn't see out of one eye, the side of her face was burning with pain; added to that she was hungry, thirsty, tired, and scared. But most of all she was angry. She didn't want to be where she was any longer. She wanted to be in bed reading a novel and eating marzipan.

She had had enough.

"Be still," she screamed at the horses. They froze in place.

Leonidas! In her mind she reached out to him, straining her gift as hard as she ever had before. *Get back here right now, you horrible beast!*

She pulled a handkerchief out of her pocket and pressed it to her left eye to staunch the bleeding. She had heard that head wounds bled worse than anything else, and now she believed it. Looking down at her coat with her good eye, she could see that she was drenched in blood.

"I look like I work in an abattoir," she muttered. Cocking her head, she couldn't hear Leonidas returning, so she snapped her fingers at Florian. "Go get him; bring him here," she ordered. "I know *you* understand. Go. Get. Leonidas. *Now.*"

Another snap of her fingers brought Bluebell to her side. The mare had a few small cuts to one knee and her chest, so Anthea pulled out her canteen and splashed water on them before pouring some on her own face. Blinking away water and blood, she looked at the other two mares.

They were standing in a huddle, their thoughts all jumbled. They seemed to be simultaneously in awe of and frightened by her.

"Good," she said.

She heard rustling behind her, and turned to see a repentant-looking Leonidas being herded by Florian. Head hanging down, Leonidas shuffled over to Anthea. She rubbed his forehead and rinsed the cuts on his legs. None of them was very deep, but he was trailing bits of wire, which had snagged in fallen branches. Anthea sighed as she hung her canteen back on Bluebell's saddle. He would never make it back to the road unless she got his legs free.

The horses all stirred as Arthur came flapping down from the branch where he had been sitting. If they bolted because of a bird, Anthea thought, a bird that they *knew*, she would . . . She couldn't think straight enough to finish the thought. Her eye felt like it was swelling, which did not bode well.

Arthur landed on the ground in front of Florian, who bent his head down and snuffled at the owl. Arthur made an angry noise and moved around Florian, straight to Leonidas. Leonidas started to sidestep, but Florian snorted and he froze.

"Come here, little one," Anthea said. "You don't want to get stepped on."

Arthur ignored her and began to nip at the wires around Leonidas's legs with his sharp beak. Anthea reached down to grab him, but just then the tiny owl bit through one of the wires and they all slithered to the ground around Leonidas's hooves, leaving him completely free.

"Oh," Anthea said. "Thank you."

He came over to her and flapped his wings just enough to get off the ground. She snatched him out of the air and put him on the pommel of Bluebell's saddle.

We are going now, she told the horses. *Back to find Jilly and Buttercup and poor Caesar.*

She turned and looked at Bluebell. Anthea pressed her handkerchief to her bloodied face one more time, and then stuck it in her pocket with a sigh.

Bluebell bent her front legs until she was low enough for Anthea to simply fall into the saddle. Once she was in place, Bluebell stood with a proud shake of her mane.

"You are a good girl," Anthea said, her voice thick. She stroked Bluebell's neck. *The best of mares. My favorite mare.*

She reached out a hand to Leonidas, and when he came close enough she grabbed his bridle and then his reins and tied them to Bluebell's saddle. He was hurt and skittish, and if he took it into his head to bolt again she wasn't sure even Florian would be able to catch him.

Bring the others, she instructed Florian.

She nudged Bluebell with a heel and headed her through the trees toward the road, with Leonidas trailing behind Bluebell, and Florian herding the other mares like a collie dog with a flock of sheep.

When the bullet ripped through her side, Anthea honestly didn't understand what had happened. The sound of the shot didn't come for another heartbeat, and to their credit, the horses didn't panic.

Which was good, since Anthea fell right in front of Florian's hooves.

FLORIAN

Florian would never forget the sight of his Beloved Anthea falling to the ground. She didn't cry or scream, but simply fell.

Everything stopped. Every horse froze. The foolish little owl, who had been on the front of the mare Bluebell's saddle, flew silently to a tree and perched there, watching with his round eyes.

Then came a man's voice, shouting that he had caught them at last. Shouting that the wretched deer would not ruin his barley, not this year. And then the men burst through the trees, and stopped, and there was silence once more, for perhaps a pair of heartbeats.

There were three men, with rough voices, carrying guns. Two of them began to talk at the same time, one to wonder, loudly and coarsely, what kind of beasts they had caught, the other to shout that he had shot a person.

At this, Florian moved forward so that he was standing over his Beloved, guarding her as The Thornley had taught him to guard a fallen rider. Although she was not trained to fight, the mare Juniper came up on his flank, placing herself between the men and Florian. The mare Bluebell turned so that she was facing the men and Florian both.

What can we do? she asked.

The men continued to shout and rail, but they moved no closer, so Florian and his herd ignored them. The owl flew to another branch and looked back at Florian, expectant. From the tattered leaves and twigs, Florian could see that it was the way they had come.

Perhaps the owl was as smart as Beloved Anthea claimed.

Florian looked gravely at Leonidas.

Because of your foolish and headstrong behavior, she who is most beloved of mine is injured, he said.

Leonidas hung his head.

Now we must get her back onto this noble mare, Bluebell, and carry her to She Who Was Jilly. The owl will help to lead us.

At this last Leonidas raised his head in astonishment.

Forgive me, the mare Bluebell said. *But my back is narrow, and the smell of blood is filling me with fear. Perhaps the Anthea . . . Beloved Anthea . . . should ride upon you, Florian.*

The other horses quickly agreed, and there was no more time. The men were moving slowly toward them. Their shock at seeing Florian and the other horses had faded, been replaced with a curiosity that Florian did not like.

Florian moved back so that he was not above his Beloved. The smell of blood clogged his nostrils, and he was filled with rage. A twig cracked beneath a man's boot and Florian snapped his teeth at the men, who drew back, but not far.

Beloved Anthea groaned. She moved feebly, like a new foal. Florian went to his knees beside her. He nudged at her with feelings of love and the mare Bluebell grabbed Beloved Anthea's collar with her strong teeth and helped to raise her up.

"Florian," Beloved Anthea whispered.

She slumped onto his back. Her feet did not find the stirrups. She grabbed a painful handful of mane as well as the knotted reins.

"My love, my love, do not forsake me," Beloved Anthea whispered.

Go! Florian ordered his herd.

They ran.

25

Red Silk Roses

THEY FOUND THE ROAD easily enough. The horses had gone straight across the fields, moving from a trot to a rolling gallop once they left the trees, despite Anthea's distressed gasps and Leonidas's groans. But she was too frightened of the hunters and in too much pain to make a fuss.

Her left side was on fire, and every step Florian took sent a jolt of agony through her. She didn't know if the bullet had gone through or was still in her side, but the bleeding seemed to have slowed. She dragged off her scarf and wadded it against her side, holding it in place under her coat with her elbow. She clutched Florian's mane and reins with her right hand and prayed that none of the horses would panic and that the men wouldn't start shooting.

They were still behind the horses, stalking them. They

seemed to think that Anthea wasn't human, calling for their dogs and talking openly of capture, of the best place to shoot "a monster" without hurting it, as though she weren't there, as though she couldn't hear their coarse voices.

They made it to the road, and then Anthea had to figure out where to go. Which way had Jilly gone with that farmer? Anthea could not remember passing a farmhouse before they ran into the tractor, so it must lie to the south.

"That's good," she said aloud. "We want to go south."

Then Anthea started to cry. They were so close! So close to Bell Hyde, and the queen, and finishing their stupid, stupid quest! But she was shot, and blinded with her own blood, and Leonidas and Caesar were both hurt. Anthea wanted to run to the nearest farmhouse and beg for aid, but surely that was where the hunters had come from. It was all Anthea could do not to turn around and flee back to the Last Farm. Let Jilly have her glory, let her ride in triumph to the queen's palace with a string of mares; Anthea just wanted to rest.

Behind them, the men who had shot her were halfway across the field. One of them began hooting and calling for the "monsters" to stop, while another argued loudly that they would still be a catch if they were dead. Anthea weakly urged her charges forward on the hard, clear road. *Faster, faster. Don't stop until we find Jilly.*

But apparently finding Leonidas and not being killed by hunters had used up Anthea's quota of heavenly blessings that day. After half an hour they still saw no sign of Jilly or the broken tractor, which meant they were already past the one safe farm. Anthea looked for a place where they could at least hide, an old barn or a copse of trees, but there were no more breaks in the hedges, only endless green walls with endless green fields behind them.

The road curved, which at least hid them from view for a little while, and as they came around it they saw someone, but it was not their kind farmer, nor was it some casual farmwife carrying eggs or a child loitering on the way home from school.

No, they came around the bend in the road, and through her one good eye Anthea saw a motorcar complete with liveried driver. The driver was leaning against a low stone fence just behind the car, smoking, and facing Anthea and her horses. As soon as he saw them he straightened and tossed down his cigarette.

"Milady," he called, but not at Anthea, whose foggy mind experienced a momentary confusion. He turned instead to his passenger.

Anthea blinked her good eye, wondering if she was feverish. In the backseat of the motorcar sat an elegant lady, her wide-brimmed hat swathed with veils. She wore a dove-gray driving coat that perfectly fit her slender shoulders, and at the sound of her driver's voice she stood and turned around, revealing a tall, trim figure that looked as completely out of place on the rough country road as Anthea and her horses.

"Here they come," the man said, jerking his chin at Anthea and her herd. "But there's just the one."

"It's the right one," the woman said. "Excellent!"

Anthea sat back and Florian stopped. The other horses clustered around her.

Behind them she could hear the pounding of the hunters' feet. Ahead of them was this car. She thought of how Uncle Andrew had told her that the horses were trained to fight. She wondered how effective they would be against shotguns and motorcars.

Her side hurt so badly that she thought she might vomit, and the cut above her eye was seeping blood again. If the woman so much as frowned at her, she was going to tell Florian to attack. She didn't know what else to do.

The woman stepped slowly down from the motorcar. Her hat was the size of a wagon wheel, navy straw with red silk roses all around the brim, and cream-colored veiling. Stupidly, Anthea remembered that she had planned to pick roses to decorate the horses' bridles before they left Last Farm. She had hoped people would think that they were on an errand *for* the queen, not just *to* her, and . . .

"Oh," Anthea said as the meaning of the roses on the woman's hat struck her.

As the woman lifted her veils, Anthea could more clearly see the gold rose pinned to her lapel. She was very beautiful, perhaps forty years old, her face lightly powdered and her lips painted red. She had dark hair and a small mole at the corner of her smiling mouth.

"Anthea," she said warmly. "I can't believe how grown-up you are, my darling!"

"Who are you?" Anthea asked. Her voice was thick and strange.

"Don't be rude," the driver snapped. "We've been waiting hours."

"Why?" Anthea asked, confused.

For a fleeting moment she thought that Jilly had sent them back to get her. But she couldn't possibly imagine this woman living anywhere near a farm. And hadn't the farmer said there were no motorcars here?

"Get into the car, darling," the woman said. "You look done in! You can rest while Stephen drives."

"What?" Anthea's head was swimming. "Who?"

"Now, will the horses follow? Which one is Florian?" The woman looked at them with her head tilted. "I never could tell a chestnut from a bay; your father despaired of me! Get in the car, darling, and tell Florian to bring the others."

The woman restored her veils and then climbed back into her seat. The driver came cautiously toward Anthea, holding up his hands.

"I'll help you, miss," he said.

"Who is she? What's going on?" Anthea demanded.

"The lady's name is not your business," the driver said. "But if she tells you to get in her car, you get in her car!"

He grabbed hold of Anthea's waist to lift her down and she

screamed. The man let out a curse, shouted it into her ear, actually. From behind her there came the sound of thudding boots, and a shotgun being cocked.

Anthea did the only thing she could do, under the circumstances, and fainted again.

26

THE ROYAL TRAIN

WHEN ANTHEA WOKE SHE thought that her body had turned to wood. She couldn't move. She wanted to scream, but she thought that if she opened her mouth and no sound came out, either, she would go completely mad.

Then she realized that she was frantically wiggling her fingers and toes.

"Oh!"

And her voice did work after all.

She moved her head then, and found that she could. There was a thin line of heat near her left eyebrow, and with a moan she remembered the wire from the snare cutting her face. She envisioned an angry red scar slicing across her face and gave another moan.

"Are you awake at last?"

Anthea turned her head and saw an elegant woman sitting in the chair beside her bed. She was reading a book, which she set aside when she met Anthea's gaze.

The woman's cream linen suit sparked a memory in Anthea's fuzzy brain. Then she saw the gold rose brooch on her lapel and everything came flooding back.

Anthea tried to say something, but her throat was so parched that she could only squeak another "Oh!"

"Here, drink this," the Rose Matron said.

She lifted a glass of water from the bedside table. To Anthea's mortification it had a spoon in it, and the woman fed her a spoonful of water.

Once the water was in her mouth, however, Anthea realized that a spoonful was the most she could swallow. And it wasn't until she had had three spoonfuls that she felt she could really talk, although she still couldn't move her arms and legs. Of the many questions she had, that became the most urgent.

"We had to tie you down so that you wouldn't injure yourself further," the woman explained. "Though I suppose I could undo you now."

She adjusted something on the side of the bed, and the pressure across Anthea's chest was released. She lifted her arms and looked at her hands: they seemed fine, if pale and shaky. The woman released her legs, and Anthea rolled her ankles a little, then she struggled to sit up.

"You shouldn't move until you're used to the motion of the train," the woman said.

"The train?"

And now that she wasn't tied down, Anthea felt her body swaying slightly. She sat up on her elbows and saw that she was in a train car, albeit one decorated like a lady's bedroom. The trees flashing by the windows made it clear that they were moving, and swiftly.

"Where am I . . . ? How long have I . . . ? What is going on?"

"You were shot, I brought you onto my private train to take care of you," the woman said. "I removed the bullet myself and stitched up your face." She clucked her tongue. "It will leave a scar, but that can't be helped."

Bits of images came rushing back: the tractor. Caesar's injury. Leonidas in the snare. The bullet wound in her side.

"Where are they?"

Anthea felt a pang. She should have asked about the horses immediately when she woke! Leonidas's cuts . . . and Florian! Was Florian safe?

She said this last aloud. She quickly sent out a thought to them: *Don't be afraid, my brave ones. I'm coming for you!*

"The horses? They are well," the Rose Matron said. She shook her head as though this was of no importance. "We put them in one of the cars near the rear. I was not prepared for an entire herd, though I assumed you would have Florian with you, so they have some food, and plenty of water."

"How do you know his name?"

Anthea sat straight up. Her head spun a little, but she ignored it. There was a startled flapping from the foot of the bed, and now Anthea saw that her clothes had been neatly folded onto a bench there, and Arthur was on top of it. She snapped her fingers and he flew at once to her lap.

"Ah, yes. The owl," the woman said. "Quite the menagerie, I must say!"

"I need to see them," Anthea said. "My horses."

"You're white as a ghost. Why don't you lie down again and—"

"I need to see them. *Now*," Anthea interrupted.

She tried to swing her legs over the side of the bed, but her wounded side sent her a furious message. Anthea hissed with pain and grabbed at the bedclothes.

"Don't you dare take that tone with me, young lady!"

"Who *are* you?" Anthea demanded.

The Rose Matron threw back her head and laughed. "I suppose it would be too much to ask that you remember me. But really, my dear, I thought you would have guessed!" She smiled at Anthea. "I'm your mother, of course."

∽✖∼

When Anthea awoke for the second time on the train, she didn't need a moment to remember where she was. Everything came rushing back at once, culminating in the elegant Rose Matron announcing that she was Anthea's mother. Anthea didn't feel embarrassed for lying back down and going to sleep after that revelation. She was injured, after all, and really: What else could she have done?

It did take her a moment to figure out why she had woken up, but then Arthur gave her ear a particularly hard nip. Feeling her ear, she didn't think he had been chewing on it for long, but she gave him a stern tap on the beak anyway.

She was alone in the lovely bedroom, and this time she found sitting up and drinking water painful but still possible. Then she pushed aside the blankets and tried to get out of bed. The world tilted, more than the movement of the train warranted, but by holding on to the bed rail she was able to manage.

Anthea found herself in a starched white nightgown, edged with so much lace that it covered her hands, and long enough to drag on the ground. Her clothes were neatly folded, but still filthy, and there was a silk dressing gown hanging on the hook by the window.

As she slowly pulled it on over her nightgown, she gazed out the window. Fields were rushing by, but they could have been anywhere. Bell Hyde might have been just around the bend, or they might have been back in the north for all Anthea could tell.

It was morning, and the glass was still chilled. Anthea's breath fogged the glass. Before it could dissipate she wrote her name with a shaking finger. Then she put Arthur in the pocket of the dressing gown and fumbled her way out.

Anthea managed to stagger across the walkway and into the next car, which was decorated like a combination sitting and dining room. The end Anthea stood in had a sofa, occasional tables strewn with magazines and books, and lamps with stained glass shades. Beyond the sofa was a dining table, set for two, and standing beside it speaking to a waiter, was her mother.

The waiter saw Anthea first, and his eyes widened. Her mother finished what she was saying, and waited for him to go out the door at the far end before turning.

"Darling, you should be in bed!"

"I'm fine," Anthea lied, gripping the back of the chair in front of her to remain upright.

"At least sit down," her mother urged.

Anthea walked around the chair and fell into it, which sent a jolt of pain through her side and made her gasp. Her face was also throbbing dully where it had been cut and then stitched. There had been a mirrored dressing table in the bedroom car, but Anthea had been too scared to look.

Her mother came around the sofa and took the chair nearest to hers. She put out a hand and squeezed Anthea's knee, still smiling with great delight.

"I can't believe it's really you, my darling!" she said. "After all these years!"

"Yes," Anthea said. "It has been a long time. Why?"

A sob was trying to push its way up Anthea's throat. She suddenly longed to squeeze into her mother's chair and put her arms around her. Anthea put one hand on the arm of her chair, ready to stand up and move, when Arthur struggled out of her pocket and settled on her knees with an annoyed hoot.

Anthea breathed deeply. She looked at the rose on her mother's lapel. It was gold with a ruby at the center, like Belinda Rose's but considerably larger. It was pinned to the same place where Anthea had pinned her own silver-and-pearl pendant.

"Why did you leave me?" Anthea asked again.

"Darling, I had to," her mother said. "I know it makes me seem like such a beast! But you see, even after my marriage I was needed by the Crown. I never retired to the life of high teas and garden parties like Deirdre. His Majesty needed me far too much!" She gave a little laugh and glanced away, exactly the way Miss Miniver taught you should when receiving a compliment.

Anthea started to raise her eyebrows but it hurt, so she smoothed her face and didn't show any expression as she asked, "Did you know that I thought you were dead?"

"Oh, no! Really?" Her mother put her hands to her cheeks. "How awful!"

"I suppose it was naïveté on my part," Anthea said. "No one actually told me you were dead, but when they told me my father died in a train crash, I assumed that you and he would have been together."

"Oh, poor Charles!" Her mother waved a hand in front of her face. "Let's not speak of it!"

"All right," Anthea said.

She found that she had to concentrate very hard on her breathing. If she breathed too deeply, it hurt her wound. But if her breathing was too shallow, she felt dizzy. Breathing just the right amount, however, required her to focus not just on her lungs and ribs, but also on the words she was saying.

"Then why now? Why after more than ten years have you come for me?"

"Pure maternal luck," her mother said. She leaned forward and stroked Anthea's hair away from her face. "There I was, going about my business, as I have sworn to the king that I shall, when I stumble upon my only daughter—"

Anthea frowned.

"But you were waiting for me."

"What's that?" Her mother frowned as well. "Oh no! Stephen had to stop for a cigarette, and I was consulting a map when you—"

"You weren't surprised to see me," Anthea insisted. Her memories were coming clearer. "Stephen said you were waiting. You knew *Florian's* name."

"So clever!" her mother said, smiling with her full red lips, but not her eyes. "Well, I was traveling, and the last village I stopped at mentioned seeing a girl with horses, a brown-haired girl with a rose on her jacket. Who else could it have been?"

Anthea didn't say anything.

"Did you really think I wasn't keeping an eye on you? My only child?" Her mother laughed. "Oh, darling, I have watched over you most anxiously! I've seen how your relatives shuffle you about, and I knew the very day that you were sent back to Andrew, and Florian."

Anthea tried to raise her eyebrows again but stopped herself in time.

"Oh yes, I know all about Florian! Your father's great experiment, to see how closely bonded horse and rider could be!" Her mother plucked idly at the fringe on a cushion. "It seems to have worked, too, judging from the beast's reaction to your fainting."

Anthea felt a sudden thrill at that. She and Florian, meant to be together, bonded closer than any other horse and rider. But all the same she kept her face blank. This was not how she had imagined meeting her mother, when she had learned her mother was still alive.

"You let my father experiment on me?" Anthea asked. "Your only child?"

"Goodness, Anthea, you make me feel like I was some sort of stage villain!" Her mother fanned her cheeks. "Your father loved you as much as he loved his horses; he would never have done anything to hurt you! He wanted to test that foolish Leanan superstition . . . what is it?"

"The Way?"

"That's right." Her mother shook her head ruefully. "Speaking to dumb animals! Nonsense, and yet . . ." She gestured at the far door, beyond which the horses waited, and then at Arthur.

Anthea did not bother to defend the Way. She did not have the strength. Instead she scooped up her owl in one hand, and used the other to haul herself to her feet.

"I would like to see my horses now," she announced.

Her mother didn't argue but instead led her through the train car, across the walkway to another car that housed the kitchen and the laundry. The staff looked up, startled, as mother and daughter passed through. Then they entered a large, unfurnished compartment that held the motorcar at the near end, and at the far end . . .

"Florian!"

He was standing at the front of the group, the mares and Leonidas behind him. They looked like they were ready for an attack, but Anthea could see that Florian's head was drooping, and she could feel how exhausted he was.

When she called his name, however, he snapped to attention and greeted her with a gentle whicker. All the horses perked up, ears flicking forward as Anthea greeted them.

My good, brave darlings! I am here!

Anthea somehow found the energy to run to them, nearly crushing Arthur as she threw her arms around Florian's neck.

Yes, Florian was tired, they were all tired, and sore, and scared. And Bluebell was hurt now as well as Caesar and Leonidas. Anthea pulled Arthur out of her pocket and plopped him on Florian's back to keep him out of the way as she pushed between the horses to look at Bluebell, who was leaning against the back wall of the train car.

"She's been shot," Anthea said in a daze.

"Yes," her mother said. "There was a pack of locals

following you down the road. I think they wanted to keep the horses, or sell them as a curiosity. They even followed us to the train, howling that the animals were their property now. One of them fired off a shot just as we were loading you all in." She rolled her eyes.

Anthea looked at the angry red furrow running across the top of Bluebell's rump where the bullet had plowed up the skin as it passed over her. It didn't need stitches, but it was no doubt painful.

"I'm so sorry," she whispered. "My brave girl!"

She looked back at her mother, who was still standing near the door. Her mother looked mildly amused, if anything.

"I'll need to see to Bluebell's wound, and also check Leonidas's cuts and—"

"Oh, does it really matter? They're just animals!"

Anthea clenched her fists in Bluebell's mane. Juniper nuzzled at her hair. Leonidas butted Anthea in the shoulder, his usually prickly thoughts smoother now. And all the while Florian stood beside her, stoic and full of love.

"We're going south, aren't we?" Anthea asked without turning.

"Yes, why?"

"You will need to drop us at the train depot outside of Bellair."

"Oh, we're already past that," her mother said. "We're almost to Travertine!"

"Travertine?"

"Oh yes," her mother said. "The king himself has asked to see you."

Anthea shook her head. "No, I need to meet up with Jilly and get to Bellair. Well, to Bell Hyde."

"Oh, you're off to see the *queen*," her mother sneered. "And her charming little country home!"

Startled by the venom in her mother's voice, Anthea finally turned around. Her mother was fingering the rose on her lapel, but her red-painted smile had turned nasty.

"I'm afraid that's not possible," she said. "We really must get you to Travertine. The king is very interested in you, Anthea, which is why he sent me to get you. On his private train, no less!"

Anthea blinked several times. "How does the king know about me? How did you know where to find me?"

Her mother waved a hand, elegantly brushing aside her questions. "I broke with the queen some years ago, you see," she said, as lightly as though reporting that she had changed hairdressers, "and I went to work for the king.

"And now he wants you to work for him as well."

FLORIAN

Beloved Anthea was pressed against Florian's flank. He was pleased that she was with him, but her emotions were a great turmoil. He did not like the train or the motorcar or the woman who smelled of dying roses.

The Rose Woman talked about kings and crowns, things that Florian did not concern himself over. Anthea was shaking her head slightly, but then she stopped and held very still. Florian willed himself to be still, despite the rocking of the train.

Florian, his Beloved said into his mind. It was clearer than any thought he had ever had from a human, almost as clear as another horse's voice.

Beloved, he said.

Florian, she said with greater confidence. *We must find Jilly and Buttercup.*

We have traveled so far in this machine.

I know, my darling, I know. But could you call to them? Tell them to keep going?

I do not know the mare.

Caesar is with her.

He is stubborn.

Not as stubborn as Leonidas, Beloved Anthea reminded him. *You are my herd stallion, darling Florian. I need your help.*

I have never been one before, he confessed, ashamed.

She stroked his neck. She also patted the owl, who was sitting on his poll. Her hand froze again.

Florian! Can you speak to Constantine?

Yes. He is my herd stallion.

Florian! Tell Constantine that we are in trouble! Can he tell Finn that we left Jilly on the Derrytown road? Can you do that?

I can try.

Try, my darling! Try!

The Great Train Escape

ANTHEA'S HEAD SNAPPED UP. "What did you just say?"

Her mother frowned. "Anthea, are you listening to me?"

"Not really," Anthea admitted. "I'm worried about Bluebell," she added hastily. "I need to clean the wound and cover it before it becomes infected." She did feel guilty that she hadn't gotten started on this sooner, but now caring for Bluebell would give her more time to think.

"I think it's wonderful how attached you are to them," her mother said, sounding as though the opposite were true. "And of course I understand that you must keep Florian. But with so few of them left, and after all the trouble I've gone to, to have you join me now that you're old enough? Well, you understand." Her mother moved her hands in a graceful gesture, as though urging Anthea to finish the thought.

"The trouble you've gone to?"

Her mother actually blushed and lowered her eyes demurely. When Anthea said nothing, Genevia looked up. A flash of irritation crossed her face and was gone again.

"Your letter?" Her mother opened her eyes wide, expectant. "Making sure that fool Daniel got it into the right hands?"

Anthea felt cold. She started to shake. Her mother had been lying to her all along: Genevia *had* been waiting for her on that road, the driver had said so. She had called Anthea "clever." Here they were, reunited, and first her mother had lied to her, and now that she was telling the truth it was even more horrible.

"Why would you do that?" Her voice sounded dull. She remembered what Perkins had said before, about her mother running out of information to feed the Crown. "Why use my letter? Why not just tell the king yourself? And why now?"

When I was finally happy, she added in her mind.

"Among other reasons, because I knew it was the best way to get you away from the farm. After all those years of Andrew fighting to get you back, I felt that the surest way was to have you be the one who spoiled their big secret."

She was so beautiful that Anthea wanted to cry. Genevia Cross-Thornley was even more perfect than Anthea had imagined her mother could be. Beautiful. Elegant. Shining like a diamond. But the things she said were so terrible.

"I hadn't planned on bringing you to live with me for another year," Genevia went on, "but after Deirdre had the vapors over her pregnancy, and they sent you to Andrew, I had to move matters ahead. Your letter was very helpful, by the way."

"I wish I had never written it," Anthea blurted out.

"Oh, nonsense! Aren't you excited to come with me? To live in luxury? I thought you wanted to be a Rose Maiden?"

"I do . . . I did," Anthea said, confused. She looked at the rose on her mother's jacket. "But you're not one anymore."

"Yes, but it makes an excellent disguise."

"And . . . and I would rather be at Last Farm."

"And be some sort of . . . *Horse* Maiden?" Her mother laughed, a glorious, tinkling sound.

"Why not?" Anthea felt her heart swelling. A Horse Maiden. That is what she was!

Florian stamped a foot, Leonidas threw up his head. Anthea stroked their necks, soothing them. *Be calm for now, all of you . . . we'll find a way out of here.*

"Why not? You silly girl!" Her mother got her voice under control. "Because your father's family and their foolish nostalgia for these animals is just that . . . foolish. Once you join me in Travertine, you'll see. You'll see my beautiful house, the ways in which His Majesty rewards me—this is the *royal train*! And it is always at my disposal!"

"You live in Travertine?"

She realized that even six months ago she would have been starry-eyed at the promise of a luxurious life in Travertine. But now it just seemed so . . . pointless. Was her mother really so shallow that she had abandoned her own child just for a big house and fine clothes? Anthea couldn't bear to think about it.

"Yes, though I have other residences, by the seaside, in Bellair—"

Anthea began to stroke Florian's neck with greater intensity. She couldn't block out her mother's words, and began to wonder how close to Uncle Daniel her mother lived. How close to bitter Aunt Anne. All that time alone, being teased by Belinda Rose, being shuffled from house to house, and Anthea's mother had been a few streets away, waiting until she was "old enough" to be worth her time.

"Really," her mother went on, musingly, "it's nostalgia on my part, I suppose, that I didn't do something about that farm years ago. But your father loved it so. I can't understand why; I think the Ice Fields probably have a more thriving culture." She shuddered. "I never was sure if the queen arranged our marriage as revenge for my working with her husband or because she thought it would win me over to her cause."

"What's the queen's cause?" Anthea asked.

Her mother's gaze sharpened. Her faintly amused smile vanished. "Enough babbling! Now you must rest!"

Anthea nodded. There was no reason to deny it. She felt like she might faint again, just so she could lie down. Only Florian and Juniper were holding her up.

But when her mother turned to leave, Anthea did not

follow. "I need to see to the horses," she said, wishing that her voice sounded stronger.

"Very well," her mother said. "Don't be too long. I will tell the cook that we are ready for dinner."

When the door shut, Anthea turned at once to Florian.

She started to pull a spare shirt out of his saddlebags, but she didn't have the willpower to get dressed. Instead she unbuckled the straps and let the bags thud to the floor. Then she slid Bluebell's saddle off the poor mare's back. There was no time to bandage her wound, it would have to wait. Anthea untied the lead lines and looped them over the horses' necks, knotting them to their saddles so they wouldn't trip over them.

"Listen," she said to them when she was ready. "Florian is your herd stallion."

Florian is your herd stallion, she repeated. *You will follow him. And me. We are going to jump out of this train, and we are going to find Jilly. And Buttercup and Caesar and Campanula.* She knew the horses' names would mean more than Jilly's. *No matter what: Follow Florian, find Buttercup and Caesar and Campanula.*

She took hold of Florian's bridle and pulled his face in close to hers. She could feel his hot breath blowing on her neck and see the worry in his eyes. To her surprise, tears filled her eyes and began to roll down her cheeks.

"My love, my love, do not forsake me," she said.

She went to the wooden door of the train car and studied

it. It opened like a drawbridge, doubling as a ramp to drive the motorcar up and down. On one side it had a simple latch that Anthea lifted, making the door rattle. On the other side it was secured with a padlock that pulled and clanked as the train moved.

Anthea studied the car next. It was the exact model that Miss Miniver drove.

Knowing that her mother could be back at any moment, Anthea moved quickly. She took Florian's heaviest saddlebag and stuffed it in front of the driver's seat. She adjusted the wheel, the clutch, and released the brake.

Then she hit the starter and leaped back.

The car roared to life. It shot forward at an angle, ramming the side of the door where the lock was. With a horrifying squeal, the padlock broke. The door slammed open, bouncing and scraping at the ground as they raced along, and the car roared down it to crash into the trees.

Florian caught Anthea as she fell back. He bent his knees and rolled his shoulder, and she was on his back. She hiked up her nightgown and dressing gown, made sure that Arthur was safe in her pocket, and squeezed Florian with her knees.

He needed no further urging. Just as the door into the train car banged open, Florian staggered down the shuddering ramp with the other horses struggling along at his heels and Anthea clinging to his back.

Florian surged through the trees, getting out of sight of the train, and Anthea stuck low to his neck even though it pained her wounded side. When they could no longer see the train behind them, Anthea tried to turn Florian to the south, toward Bellair, but Florian would not turn.

Finally Anthea stopped fighting him and let him stop. The other horses crowded around her, and she reached out a shaking hand to each of them.

You are wonderful, so wonderful, my darlings! she told them.

Bluebell was not doing well, but she lovingly blew on Anthea's knee when Anthea stroked her and brushed her forelock out of her eyes.

"We have to go to Bellair," Anthea said.

Florian turned north and west. He whinnied, and Anthea caught an image of Buttercup in her mind. She remembered her mother's words: they were past Bellair already.

"Oh," she said. *That is my good, brave boy,* she said to Florian. *Now find Jilly!*

28

MIGHTY LONG ROAD

ANTHEA DID NOT BECOME aware of the rain until it had soaked her through. She had a vague sense that she had a fever, which had started not long after they had found the road. The rain cooled her fever, at first, which was good. But then she began to shiver, which was not good. That was when she began to notice her surroundings and the chill wetness of her scant clothing.

"Florian." Her voice was little more than a croak. *Florian, are we on the right road?*

He nodded and sent her the reassuring image of Buttercup and Jilly. She sagged in the saddle again, relieved.

Leonidas, hovering at her knee, whickered anxiously and nudged the reins.

She realized, after a moment of shock, that he was worried

that she was angry with him. Also, it bothered him that she was not holding Florian's reins. She took them in her chilled hands and he relaxed, his head rising and his small, pointed ears flicking forward.

"You are a strange beast," she croaked at him. "I'm still not sure I like you."

His head went down, and she felt a pang of guilt.

Her throat was so dry it felt like every word scratched and left a scar inside her mouth. She opened her mouth to the rain as it poured down. She even put the tail of her sopping-wet hair in her mouth and sucked some of the moisture out of it. It tasted like sweat as well as rain, and she shuddered. Then she began shaking so hard that she feared that she would rattle herself right off Florian's back.

"Miss Miniver, you should see me now," she said through chattering teeth.

Dropping the reins again, she hugged herself. She was cold and wet, hot and parched at the same time. The steady throbbing of her side, in time to her heartbeat, had been going on so long that she no longer noticed it unless a particularly hard shiver made the muscle twinge.

She hunched over and put her arms around Florian's neck.

Florian, I'm dying.

His ears went back and he began to walk faster.

I won't make it to Bell Hyde.

He began to jog. She made a small noise of protest at the

jostling, and he went even faster until he was moving at a nice, smooth lope.

Anthea settled into this new pace. It made the rain stream back along her cheeks and cool them a little. It was like being rocked, too, and she let her eyes fall closed. Rocked. She remembered her mother rocking her, singing—no, not her mother: her father. Her father had rocked her to sleep, and sung to her.

"Hush 'bye, 'bye, don't you cry," Anthea sang brokenly. "Go to sleep, ye little babby. When you wake, you'll have sweet cake, and all the pretty little horsies."

That was all she could manage, and then it made her cough. When the coughing abated, she thought of Jilly, singing as they had ridden along on their exciting mission. Before the tractor, before Leonidas in the snare, before the bullet in her ribs and the one that gouged Bluebell. Before her mother.

Jilly's exuberance that day seemed to be years ago now. And her own unease over . . . what? That someone would see her wearing trousers, riding a horse? Who would care what she wore? Or if she rode a horse or kissed a boy? Or was shot or died of a fever on the side of the road?

"Only you, my Beloved," she whispered to Florian.

She remembered Jilly's song again.

"My love, my love, do not forsake me," she whispered to Florian. "My love, my love, do not forsake me."

Florian began to run.

FLORIAN

Beloved Anthea's thoughts were muddled, her emotions dull. Sickness came from her in waves.

When she began to fall sideways, Florian neighed in terror. Leonidas immediately pushed himself against Florian's shoulder, taking some of Beloved Anthea's weight to halt her fall.

Florian continued to run.

Leonidas matched his stride perfectly. Although broader in build, he was the same height and length of leg as Florian. They were able to run in tandem, with Beloved Anthea half lying on Leonidas's back, her legs loose on either side of Florian.

If Beloved Anthea falls— Florian began.

She will not fall, Leonidas interrupted.

Florian felt a rush of gratitude toward Leonidas.

The mares, too, called encouragement from their place

behind Florian. They kept their pace well, so that Florian had no need to worry about them. The mare Holly said that she would keep pace with the injured mare Bluebell, should she fall behind, and they would come after. The mare Juniper said she had neither fear nor tired legs, and to go at greater speed if needed.

So Florian ran.

He ran until his heart pounded and his lungs screamed for air. He ran until each hoofbeat sent a shock up his legs. Beloved Anthea had her hands wrapped painfully in his mane as well as the reins so that she did not fall off, but her body was too loose on his back, filling him with greater fear. Leonidas called out that they must slow down, even as he continued to keep pace with Florian. The others cried out their sorrow, but they could run no farther. Florian left them behind.

He called out to Constantine, telling him to come, swiftly, and collect the mares. Telling him to bring the Soon King, and gather their scattered herd, because Florian could not.

Florian was not a good herd stallion.

He was the Beloved of his Beloved, and he would not forsake her.

29

MIGHTY LONG RIVER

ANTHEA WAS ON A boat, drifting, drifting, drifting down a river. Sometimes the current ran fast and jolted her, other times it was slow and smooth. She wanted to lie back and let the boat carry her along while she slept, but it didn't seem possible.

Noises kept intruding: guns firing, or perhaps that was thunder. Was there a storm? In this hot weather? No, it was raining Then why was she so hot?

Leonidas kept prodding her with his nose, and Arthur landed on her head and bit her ear several times. She swatted them away. She needed to sleep, couldn't they leave her alone for one minute to sleep?

She was terribly thirsty, too, but couldn't seem to reach over the side of the boat and dip out a handful of water. Whenever she summoned the strength to do so, Leonidas shoved her arm back. Awful animal! Why did he hate her so?

This went on for months, or years. It was hard to be sure. There was no night or day, only an endless twilight, golden and gray and always peaceful.

She was slipping away at last: Florian's thoughts had quieted and Leonidas had stopped pestering her. The boat was rocking so gently that she was floating like a leaf. The twilight began to darken, shading her eyes, and she sighed with pleasure.

A loud voice cut across the darkness.

"More of them? Running around loose? Filthy things!"

"Don't be an old fool! You just— Here, now!"

There was stamping and a thud. Anthea's boat stopped moving.

"What is it?"

"There's a dead girl on this one!"

"It's the plague!"

"That's a myth!"

"Don't touch her!"

Anthea longed to tell them to be quiet but she couldn't move or talk. She could only lie there in her boat.

Was it a boat?

"Stay away from her!"

It was a voice she knew, but Anthea could not have said why. There was a thudding sound, was that thunder or . . . hooves?

"Whoa, there, Florian! It's all right, big man!"

The voice belonged to a nice person, she knew that, but he shouldn't stop the river. The river had to keep flowing.

"Let me just grab the reins . . . Stop it, Con!"

Her boat heaved as the river churned. There were strange cries. Anthea hoped she wasn't the one making them.

"Fine then! I'll lead the mares, and you follow me, Florian. We're almost there."

"Who are you?" The first voice was demanding or perhaps scared, Anthea couldn't tell.

"I'm the king of Leana," the familiar voice said. "I have business with your queen. Let us pass."

The river began to flow again, and Anthea let herself drift with it. She was so light. She didn't even worry that she couldn't move. She was a dry leaf, a dandelion puff, a feather.

She was nothing.

"There they are! There they are!"

Another familiar voice, a girl this time.

"Wait! Finn? Is that . . . *Constantine*? What are you . . . ? Anthea!"

"Let them through, Sergeant," said a woman's cool, commanding voice. "These are the rest of my guests."

"Guests, Your Majesty?"

"Thank you so much, Your Majesty."

"Thea, Thea, are you all right?"

"Of course she's not! Look at the state of her! I found her a ways down the road. Florian's half-mad, Jilly, don't touch them!"

Anthea tried to float away but she couldn't. Familiar voices battered at her. And then there were hands, too: prodding and poking; she uttered an involuntary shriek when someone tried to pull her out of her boat.

"Her arms are wrapped in the reins," said the girl's voice. "Oh, I think we'll have to cut his mane to get her fingers loose."

"Goodness," said the calm voice. "What a mess! Let's just take everyone to the little barn, Jillian, and sort them out there."

The boat rocked wildly, and Anthea whimpered. Everything hurt, from the tips of her fingers to her scalp to the bottoms of her feet.

"Oh no! Finn, look at Florian!"

"I saw," came the grim reply.

"How is he still on his feet?"

Jilly's voice pierced Anthea's heart.

She was not on a boat; she was on Florian's back. That girl was Jilly. The boy who had found her on the road was Finn.

"Florian," she whispered. *Florian.*

Once more, she felt herself moving forward, bobbing as though on the water. She knew now that it was because something was wrong: there was pain in Florian's mind. He lurched from side to side when he walked.

She refused to open her eyes and look.

They stepped into golden light. The rain stopped.

"Let her go now," Finn said, very close to Anthea. "Florian, let her go."

Warm, strong hands took hold of Anthea. Florian shuddered. He could not take another step.

"Thank you," Anthea whispered. She unclenched her fists from his mane with difficulty. *Thank you, my Beloved.*

It all went dark again.

30

HORSE MAIDEN

"YOU SEE, MY DEAR Gareth, it's just as I've tried to tell you," Queen Josephine was saying. "The Way is hardly superstition! It's a real gift, and one that may prove to be very useful."

"Now that there are horses," King Gareth said.

He did not sound at all happy about it. But then, he hadn't sounded happy about anything, in the short time he had been at Bell Hyde.

"Oh, there have always been horses," Jilly said airily, giving her head a little shake to make the plumes in her hair flutter.

Jilly wore a pale-green gown that one of the princesses had given her, but Jilly being Jilly, she had removed the sleeves and cut away the front of the skirt so that it arced to her knees. She'd wound a dark green ribbon around her waist and tied more of the ribbon around her upper arms. Her short curls were pomaded until they were stiff and shiny, and she had taken the silk that had been the front hem of her gown and wrapped it around her brow, with two ostrich plumes and a pearl brooch above her right ear. The glittering powder on her eyelids was green, and her lips were dark cherry.

She looked magnificent, and much more suited to going to a ball than having tea with the king. Or so Anthea had tried to tell her.

"Perhaps I shall ask His Majesty to dance," she had joked.

Seeing the look on Anthea's face, she had sobered, and she helped Anthea finish getting dressed.

Anthea's borrowed dress was a white silk column, the high-waisted bodice embroidered with green vines and scarlet roses. Fluttering sleeves fell to her elbows, making her arms look slender and elegant rather than too thin, and the square neckline was very flattering. Her hair was pinned in a loose chignon, adorned with garnet-studded combs from the queen's own jewel box. A small bit of silver chain could be seen along the side of her neck, but when Jilly had tried to pull it free, Anthea had flinched away.

Now, stiffly seated in the queen's favorite parlor at Bell Hyde, Anthea wished she had let Jilly make some outrageous change to her gown. Or that she had worn trousers and boots. Anything to convince herself that the king kept looking at her because of her clothes, and not because she was . . . what? The girl who had shown up half-dead last week, with a string of injured horses?

Did he know she was the daughter of his chief spy?

"I am not comfortable with the idea that this Last Farm has existed so many years within my own borders," the king said, his mouth twisting at the name of the farm, "and without my—"

"If I may interrupt, Your Majesty?" Finn said.

King Gareth made a sharp gesture with one of his thick-fingered hands. He was a stocky man who looked rather more like a farmer than a king, Anthea thought. Finn, mean-while, was wearing a suit that the queen had found for him, which fit him perfectly. His blond hair caught the light from the large windows and made him almost glow.

He looked like the only real king in the room, Anthea thought.

She also thought it interesting that the queen's curly blond hair was almost exactly the same shade. She was taller than her husband, with a buxom figure and bright blue eyes. Also rather like Finn's.

Anthea self-consciously pulled the chain out of her bodice and let her own silver horseshoe charm hang over her breast. The queen noticed, and her smile broadened.

Her Majesty fiddled with one of her earrings. They were roses like the ones on her personal crest . . . rosebuds, actually, in a perfect U-shape with a tiny crown above them.

"My family's understanding when Kalabar built his wall

was that the land north of it was ours," Finn was saying. "We were told that the Wall was to keep us safe. And our horses." He paused. "Unless that was a lie?"

King Gareth blustered for a moment and then finally ended with, "Well, I can hardly speak for my ancestor! Kalabar's been dead for nearly three centuries!"

"And for nearly three centuries my family has carried on, with the help of the Thornleys, raising the horses that are our only legacy," Finn said. His voice was firm, but Anthea could see his hands were shaking where he gripped the arms of his chair. "I fail to see how we, or the horses, are at fault if you forgot to send someone to find out if we were all dead."

"But you have to admit, the fact that no one has mentioned this farm and these animals for hundreds of years is highly suspicious." The king gave Jilly a narrow look. "Does your father bribe people for their silence, or are there threats involved? And where is Thornley, anyway?"

"My father had to stay at Last Farm to take care of the rest of the horses, and the people who depend on him," Jilly said, her voice so cold it could have frosted the windows.

Both Anthea and Jilly had gotten letters from him, however, letters passionately informing them that they were to be punished the moment they set foot back on the farm, and that said punishment would last until they were thirty. This was undercut by the tears that blurred some of the handwriting, and Finn had told them that when he had left Last Farm, Andrew had been hugging Dr. Hewett and Nurse Shannon and shouting, "They're still alive!" over and over again.

"Huh, so Thornley's afraid to face me," King Gareth said with a smirk. "Taking care of his horses, indeed." He snorted.

"Gareth! How rude!" Queen Josephine said.

Anthea felt a hot surge of anger. She squeezed Arthur, who was sitting on her knees, a little too tight, and he flapped up to sit on the arm of her chair, digging into the brocade with his claws.

"Quite the menagerie," the king muttered.

Anthea clenched her hands in her skirts. She heard her mother's voice in her ears, coolly mocking her animals, coolly talking about their lives not mattering.

Coolly talking about how the king wanted Anthea to work for him. But then this morning Anthea had met the king, and he had given no sign that he even recognized Anthea's name when they were introduced.

"Gareth, did you never think that your own family's insistence that the poor horses carry disease might contribute?" The queen had kept going. "Who wants to admit they've been near a horse, if they are shunned for it?" She shook her head, and her earrings swung. Anthea saw Jilly notice them, and her cousin's eyes widened.

"My mother knew," Anthea said, speaking for the first time since she had been introduced to the king.

Her voice sounded rusty, but that might have been because

she was still recovering. This was the most time she had spent out of bed since her arrival. She took a deep breath and her bandaged side twinged.

"My mother knew all along," she said. "She lived at Last Farm. She could have told you at any time, and she did not."

"Your mother?" The king looked at Anthea and blinked rapidly. "But I don't know your mother, do I?" he asked pointedly.

"You've met her once or twice," the queen said, a hard edge to her voice. "She *used* to be one of my Maidens."

"Was she that redhead?" The king tapped his lower lip.

"Hardly," the queen retorted.

Jilly and Finn both looked like they might explode. They had heard the whole story, in short bursts, from Anthea. So had the queen, who had been completely unsurprised by anything Anthea's mother had said or done.

"Well, how disappointing that she didn't tell me," the king said. "I do so hate it when people disappoint me."

The threat underlying his casual tone raised the hairs on the back of Anthea's neck. Was this where her mother had learned to speak so calmly of such horrible things? Or had she taught the king? Jilly cleared her throat and Anthea quickly forced herself to focus.

"The point," she said, before someone said something regrettable, "is that now you do know. I don't know why you didn't bother to look before."

Jilly gasped. Maybe Anthea would be the one to say something regrettable, she mused. She was tempted to ask, bluntly, if her mother would be fired as the king's spy for not telling him about Last Farm.

"And I don't know why my mother didn't tell . . . anyone," she added.

"She did love your father very much," the queen said, with great sincerity. "Though she was never really cut out for life on a farm."

"More like life in a mansion with a private car and train included," Jilly muttered.

Anthea took another painful breath, shaking her head a little at her cousin. "But now we have to decide how to proceed. Finn and Jilly and I had the idea of bringing some mares here for Her Majesty, the queen, as a gift, and that is still what we would like to do.

"Right, Finn?"

"That's right," he said immediately. "Campanula, Holly, and Juniper are yours, Your Majesty." He gave a little seated bow.

"Oh, how delightful! Thank you!"

The queen clapped her hands in surprise, exactly as if she hadn't spent all week sitting beside Anthea's sickbed with Jilly and Finn, hearing every detail of what they were planning. As if she hadn't already ridden Holly the day before, been thrown, and gotten back on.

"Would you mind terribly lending us a stallion, too?" she asked.

As if that hadn't already been discussed.

"Then we could start our own southern herd," she added to her husband, who looked horrified.

"Now, see here," he began. "It's one thing for me to look the other way about what goes on beyond the Wall—"

"And here at my private estate," the queen put in.

The king ignored that. Anthea had noticed that he was good at ignoring what he didn't like.

"But if we start a herd . . ." He frowned. "How many more do we need of these curiosities?"

He said "curiosities" the same way the hunters had said "monsters" as they chased Anthea and her little herd. She clenched her hands in her skirt again. Finn reached over and put a hand, gently, on hers until she relaxed.

"Don't you understand that they're more than curiosities?" Jilly said. "They're a part of the land!"

"They're useful," Anthea said, with a little cough to clear her suddenly clogged throat. "They can be *more* useful, I mean."

"We have oxen, motorcars, trains—" The king ticked these off on his fingers.

Anthea shook her head and the king stopped, astonished. Then he realized that he was letting a girl scold him, and he scowled at her.

Anthea refused to back down.

"The Way," she said quietly. "If Your Majesty has messages that need to be sent. *Sensitive* messages. By trusted couriers." She refused to use the word "spy" but had a feeling they were all thinking it.

"Two weeks ago I was all the way north of the Wall, at Last Farm," Finn chimed in. "Constantine, the king of all the horses, broke free of his paddock and came to get me. He communicated to me that there was danger to the south, that horses had been injured, that Anthea needed me. That we had to go. I got here in less time than if I had taken the train."

"Even when I was ill," Anthea said. "My Florian continued the mission. He brought me right to the gates of Bell Hyde, as instructed, even though we have never been here."

The king's scowl faded to a thoughtful look. "Horses, a network across the country . . ."

"Exactly," Queen Josephine said, beaming.

"Exactly," Finn echoed. He looked less pleased.

Anthea put her other hand atop his and gave it a little squeeze. "Do we have a choice?" she whispered.

"Now, why don't we go have a look at them?" the queen said. "They are magnificent creatures!"

She was the first to stand, but of course the king led the way out of the palace. Finn had to take over, then, and show the king to the croquet lawn that had been hastily fenced off so that the horses could use it.

Constantine had even agreed to play nice and be penned

with the others. It helped that the croquet lawn was right outside the windows of the bedrooms they had been given. Finn kept his windows open so that he could yell at Constantine from time to time.

"What's wrong with that one?" the king asked immediately upon seeing Caesar.

"He ran afoul of a tractor, poor dear," Jilly said, her teeth gritted. She went at once to rub his nose, her posture softening when she reached him. "Didn't you, silly boy?"

"And the spotty one?"

"They're called dapples," Finn said coolly. "Bluebell was shot by some men who tried to capture her."

"Leonidas was caught in a snare," Anthea said, before the king could point to the newly contrite stallion.

Leonidas came slowly to the fence, his legs shining with ointment, and Anthea pulled his ears. He snorted wetly on her bodice.

You're awful, she said lovingly to him.

"And this is Florian," Anthea went on, her voice choking just a little. "My Florian."

She reached out an arm to him, one hand still on Leonidas's forehead, and Florian came. Where branches had scraped him, his hair seemed to be growing back in the opposite direction. He was far too thin, and worst of all, there was a thick bandage across his shoulder, covering a deep gash. Anthea didn't even know where or when he had gotten it, or how.

My love, Anthea said to him. She put a hand on either cheek and gazed into his eyes. *My darling.*

Beloved, he answered. *The herd stallion wishes to leave soon. He wishes to take the New King back to the farm.* Florian hung his head. *I do not know that I am strong enough to carry you home yet.*

I would never leave you, Anthea told him.

Hello, noble Florian. The queen had come alongside them. *Will you stay awhile with your dear girl and let her teach me to ride?*

I would be honored, Beloved of Holly, he said.

Anthea gaped at Queen Josephine. The queen laughed. She pulled a thin chain from her own bodice, and flashed a tiny horseshoe charm at Anthea before tucking it away quickly.

"Now, Miss Thea, I thought you had guessed all my secrets," the queen whispered. "Especially since I thought all Rose Academies taught that I come from a small estate far to the north. And that before I married, I was a magTaran, like young Finn." Her bright blue eyes twinkled at Anthea.

"That's enough of that," the king announced. "No more whispering, and no more animals. For now." He dusted off his hands, even though he hadn't touched one of the horses. "I have much to think about." He began to stride back toward the house.

"Don't worry, we'll steer him in the right direction," the queen whispered.

"Let's all have lunch," she called to the others.

She looped her arm through Anthea's and began to lead her back. Anthea looked over her shoulder at Jilly, who gave Caesar one last pat before coming.

"If it's all right, Your Majesty," Finn said. "I need to eat quickly. I think Constantine had better have a run before he causes trouble."

"And I actually have my appetite back," Anthea said, with some surprise.

She felt a smile blooming across her face for the first time in weeks. Out of the corner of her eye, she sneaked a peek of the queen's silver chain, and her smile broadened.

"Ugh, don't talk about food," Jilly said, coming up on her other side. "I was thinking I was hungry, and suddenly in my mouth I could taste hay." She made a face.

Finn stopped dead and spun around to stare at Jilly. "You could taste hay? Just now?"

He turned to look back at the paddock. Caesar was hanging over the makeshift fence, looking longingly after Jilly. Caesar snorted and tossed his mane. Jilly sneezed and then shook her glossy curls. Finn turned to Anthea, his eyes wide.

Anthea started to laugh.

ACKNOWLEDGMENTS

This book has been on a long road.

It started as an idea I had when I was twelve and wanted a horse of my own so badly! I wrote it down in a Cabbage Patch Kids diary and hid it away, but I never forgot the basic elements of a girl, her horse, and her wicked uncle. It reemerged in my brain more than twelve years ago, as an alternate-timeline World War I story I called "Horse Brigade," and the first chapters became my go-to piece to read at sci-fi conventions. (If you have heard me read this, prior to 2017, please shoot me an email. I owe you cookies!) But it took much more work, and many, many drafts, not to mention brainstorming sessions with my awesome editor and long-suffering agent, before it became the book you hold in your hands.

So, first of all, a huge, huge thank you to Mary Kate

Castellani, my fabulous editor and the person who realized that I had signed a contract for this book years ago and then forgotten about it! Thank you, too, for the many phone calls and emails and your encouragement and enthusiasm. You are awesome!

Thank you and many hugs to Amy Jameson, my agent, who has stood by me and this book the whole way. Thank you for always knowing the best places to eat, especially where the good tacos are. And the biggest thank you for that time you read this book in an hour because something was horribly awry, only to find I had sent the wrong draft. I'm so sorry.

Special thanks to the whole darn team at Bloomsbury! You guys always make me feel like a rock star, and who doesn't like to feel like a rock star? So big hugs and air-kisses to Erica Barmash, Anna Bernard, Bethany Buck, John Candell, Beth Eller (who I think was the first one to say, You wrote a book about horses? Why have I not seen it?), Cristina Gilbert, Courtney Griffin, Melissa Kavonic, Cindy Loh, Donna Mark, Elizabeth Mason, Shae McDaniel, Brittany Mitchell, Oona Patrick, Emily Ritter, Claire Stetzer, and Ellen Whitaker! It does indeed take a lot of people to make a great book!

Thanks to my family, all of you. Yes, even the children, who have finally learned to respect my office door. Deadlines affect the whole family, and the writing of every book is unique, and uniquely crazy. But my family are all such troopers. I love each and every one of you, and not just because you are my biggest cheering section.

I always imagined that I would write something poignant in this book, some love letter to my fellow horse lovers. I did my best with the dedication, but find that I am having a stupor of thought when it comes to writing anything more, so just let me say this:

If you've ever pored over books of horse breeds, trying to decide which one is "best." If you've ever searched ads for affordable saddles, even though you don't have a horse to put one on. If you've ever wanted to go riding across a green field on the back of a horse, with the wind in your hair . . . this is your book. Yours, and mine. I'm sorry it took so long.